Contents Under Pressure

BY
ALLISON NICHOL

CONTENTS UNDER PRESSURE
BY ALLISON NICHOL

ISBN 10: 1-933113-77-4
ISBN 13: 978-1-933113-77-7

First Printing: 2008

This Trade Paperback is published by
Intaglio Publications
Walker, LA. US
WWW.INTAGLIOPUB.COM

CREDITS
EXECUTIVE EDITOR: TARA YOUNG
Cover design by Valerie Hayken, www.valeriehayken.com.
and Sheri graphicartist2020@hotmail.com.

If you ask me what I came
into this world to do,
I will tell you:
I came to live out loud.
— Emile Zola

DEDICATION

For Gay Hollahan, my greatest blessing.

And for the boys of my Provincetown summers who taught me to laugh and to live out loud.

ACKNOWLEDGMENTS

The energy and good wishes of many people went into making this book a reality, and I wish to thank them all.

First, to the women of Intaglio and to Valerie Hayken for all of their dedication to this manuscript and cover design.

To Kate Nicholson, my first reader always.

To Gay, who read every version of this book and loves me anyway.

To Julie Bowman and Kathleen Sweeney, my Irish sisters.

To all the many Wodatches, for allowing me glimpses of a happy, loving family.

To Kyle, Peyton, Rick, Gregg, John Z, and my many other Provincetown brothers who have peopled my summers and my world.

To Gregg Shapiro who always believed.

To Anne Beckman for the birthday cake story.

To the Fine Arts Work Center in Provincetown, Massachusetts, a true national treasure, for allowing me the opportunity to spend time with two of America's greatest writers. To Anne Patchett, from whom I took a class there, for telling me to keep writing and find a plot.

To Mary and David, respectively the proprietor and caretaker of the Dyer's Beach House Motel in Provincetown, where this book was written over the course of several summers. I hold room three deep in my heart.

Chapter One

A dog chases a woman into a bank. The dog gets shot first.

Drew Morgan got the call Saturday morning because there had been a string of bank robberies along the East Coast, starting in New York, on to Boston, then straight up the Cape, seventeen in all. Because the robbers moved across state lines, Washington was involved.

The latest one was in Provincetown at the tip of Cape Cod. Apparently, the robbers simply ran out of room. Drew hung up the phone, threw a few blank legal pads and two manila file folders, choked with memos, into her briefcase, and headed for the garage. She dialed the familiar number as the automatic door to exit the underground parking garage lifted. She had driven four blocks on the nearly empty streets of downtown Washington when, just at the tip of ring nine, a groggy voice finally answered.

"Shaunessey?" Drew said.

"No, just a minute."

"Figures."

"Hello?" came Stephen Shaunessey's morning voice.

"Sorry, Shaunessey. I guess I should have figured you'd still have company."

"Funny, Morgan. What the hell's going on that you're calling me at eight thirty on a Saturday morning? You know I sleep late on Saturday. Oh, my god, did you hear from Maggie?"

1

"I know you don't get out of bed till noon. How much sleeping gets done I can't speak to. And no, it's not Maggie. And quit asking me that. We got another call. This time it's Cape Cod. Provincetown to be exact. Get up, get dressed, get packed. I'm like ten blocks from my house. You and I are booked on the ten o'clock flight to Boston."

"No way. Provincetown? That's like the middle of nowhere. If it's really Provincetown, then these people are really stupid. Geez, can I get more details?"

"I don't have more details. Meet me at US Airways curbside at National no later than nine. We leave at ten. Maybe we'll have more information by then. Don't be late."

Two hours later, they were on a plane headed to Logan Airport in Boston.

"I don't get it," Stephen said from the window seat. "These girls have been busy and are real runners. Girls don't usually do multiple robberies and don't usually run. And what's up with the dog?"

"The dog is definitely not a match. Well, it may not be them. We don't know that for sure. After all, there seems to be only one woman instead of two."

"Yeah, but what are the odds that there would be three unrelated female bank robbers running around Massachusetts? Something is off with that."

"They agreed to preserve the crime scene so we should know more in about an hour." Drew glanced at her watch and set her empty Diet Coke can on the flight attendants tray. "They're sending the same evidence team down from New York. They should be there by now actually."

"Please tell me they aren't sending that Stan guy. I don't think I can take it." Stephen popped a handful of pretzels into his mouth and brushed the salt from his hands.

"You know, Stephen, you need to quit that. I don't want a repeat of what happened in New York. And neither does Turner, frankly. Your behavior with those people from the Manhattan D.A.'s office was appalling."

"Yeah, I know. But that guy was such a homophobic asshole. I could never live in New York. There are just way too many people from New York living there." Stephen was grinning his gritted—I come from a working-class family that cared about teeth—smile. His dark rust-colored hair, thick in the front, stuck out slightly on the sides, evincing a rushed gel job, and his wide green gray eyes still carried the slight fog of morning.

"Quit that. I'm telling you, if you screw it up this time, you won't be able to grin your way out of it. Turner was really pissed off about what happened in New York. And even if you don't care about that, I sure as hell do, He is the chief after all."

"Okay, okay, I'll make nice with the New Yorkers, geez."

"And the Provincetown locals. Promise me."

"Of course. Why wouldn't I be nice to the locals? I love Provincetown. God, those poor people must be freaking. What an unlikely place for a bank robbery. You think it's that little red brick bank in the middle of town?"

"I would guess so. I've never even seen another bank there, but Maggie and I always stay at Angel's in that area, so I suppose there could be another one. What a mess. I can just about imagine what's going on there about now. We're going to be walking right into the middle of chaos."

"Honest to god. By the way, if Tom Turner is so pissed off about what happened in New York, how come I didn't know about that till now? "

"Because I covered for you as usual."

"What does that mean?" Stephen asked, as the wheels touched down on the runway and the plane reversed its engines.

"We need to finish this later." Drew pulled her carry-on down from the overhead compartment. "We only have twenty minutes to make the connection to Cape Air."

Drew sat in the co-pilot seat in the tiny eight-seater Cape Air jet and stared down at the small white sailboats snaking their way along the shore. Flecks of early afternoon sunlight sparked off the inky blue water like a scattering of dimes. It was an intimate and familiar sight.

She and her lover, Maggie, had made this flight at least twice a year for the last ten. She had never made this trip without Maggie's hand closed in her own. She thought about the joy of their trip the previous summer, about this same time, this same plane probably. The gulf between that summer and this, between she and Maggie, had grown as wide as the blue beneath her.

Maggie had been gone six months, slipped away soft as a sigh. She had left a few cryptic phone messages but nothing concrete. Nothing to give away where she might be, or when or if she might return.

Drew was becoming increasingly uncertain whether the path back was still traceable. As the dunes came into view, she wondered how they had let it get this far. When had they stopped paying attention? When had the pulse of a beeper become more important than the soft curve of muscle?

Although Drew always made a halfhearted denial every time Maggie said it, Maggie was right when she told people that if it had not been for Maggie's calves, Drew would never have noticed her. They had been biology lab partners for a month. It was a class that completely confused Drew; it seemed so dreary and unnecessary. Despite that, Drew knew she had to score at least a B to keep her average up for law school. Her only hope was being paired with a science major.

The assignments were random, and she ended up with Maggie Malone. Of all things, an art major—photography. Drew could not understand how anyone could make a living taking pictures. She also assumed that Maggie was at Northwestern because she couldn't get into The Chicago Art Institute. How could anyone hope to make a living taking pictures that were not very good?

At first they were tentative with each other, painfully polite in the way that only dykes can be when each is only "sort of" sure the other is gay. They were only juniors, after all, and both products of strict Catholic upbringings so that their gaydar, long suppressed, still had a few bugs in it. Neither was willing to be the first to be wrong.

Even though they only saw each other in class, by the end of that first month, enough code words had passed between them that it was clear that each knew the other was "family." With the pressure off, and armed with that information, Maggie Malone decided that Drew Morgan was an "MHH"—Must Have Her.

Although Maggie was not all that experienced, mostly having mastered only the disassembling and reassembling of Catholic school uniforms for quick peeks and pokes and one or two more serious girlfriends, she knew it was not the smell of formaldehyde that was making her stomach jump and dive. It was this pleasurable puzzle of a woman.

It wasn't that Drew was beautiful, although she had short cropped brown hair, her firm body still showed evidence of years of high school basketball discipline, and she could be picked out in a crowd. It wasn't her brains, either, although she was really smart, or her undeniable charm, that smile. It was none of those things. Maggie was drawn to Drew's buzz. She was electric. She just knew that this was a woman who would always be going someplace, someplace really interesting.

It wasn't as if Drew didn't notice Maggie. How could she not notice Maggie? That beautiful mane of auburn hair cascading down that slim muscled back. Her unrelenting scent, the soft smell of fresh lemon every time she passed or pressed in too close to the microscope. The way the light attached itself to her. But Drew remained cautious, afraid Maggie was one of those "semester lesbians" who play at being gay, then leave in their senior year engaged to a nice guy who's in the pre-med program.

She hadn't missed the clues Maggie gave her every time they were at the lab. A hand held just too long. A soft brush of shoulders for no necessary reason. A gaze held three seconds too long. Laughing at all of her jokes—even the really bad ones. How Maggie tossed her hair from side to side and twirled it endlessly in her fingers whenever they talked.

Drew held out until about eight weeks in when Maggie decided to pull out the big guns. On a dreary Wednesday, when she should have been in her usual uniform of jeans and a sweater, Maggie walked into class five minutes late in a black silk mini-skirt, white silk blouse with three buttons open, and black high heels. She held the attention of the entire room as she slowly snaked her way

5

through the lab tables toward Drew.

Drew felt a rush of blood to her head and picked up a white towel from the counter, swinging it slowly from her outstretched arm, signaling full surrender.

The cab driver waiting outside the tiny Provincetown airport looked like an unmade bed. She bundled the three suitcases and two briefcases into the back of the yellow station wagon with ease. "Looks like you folks are stayin' a while," she said, slamming the driver's side door for the third time trying to get it to close. "Okay, where we headed?"

"The Angel Gabriel's, please," Drew said.

"Okay, be a long ride today, though. Town's real backed up. Got half of Commercial Street blocked off. Cops in from Wellfleet and Truro. We just had our first bank robbery. Heard they shot a dog, too. Hope you two brought cash. That's why they postponed the Carnival parade. Never did that before 'cept if it was hurricane. "

"Just get us as close as you can," Drew said. "We can walk a few blocks if we have to."

"We can?" Stephen said.

"You must be from New York."

"No. Why do you say that?" Drew asked.

"I'm thinkin', if I just told you we had a bank robbery here today, the first one ever, and they postponed Carnival and all, you might have some questions about it is all. So I figure since you don't and since you got all those suitcases, you must be from New York. Girls from New York always got a lotta suitcases."

"They're his suitcases. We're from D.C. And we do have a lot of questions. We're just tired, so we're in kind of a hurry to get to Angel's. Is that all right?" Drew said in a genuine and soft voice.

"Everything's all right with me. Whatever you say, D.C. I'll get ya as close as I can as fast as I can."

Drew and Stephen could see Angel, and some of the muscular young women who worked the summers for her, waiting at the entrance, as they walked up the winding brick path to the main part of the complex. It looked the same as it had the previous summer, every summer. The small complex of two-story cedar-shingled buildings was surrounded by beautiful gardens in late summer bloom; faint fingers of steam from the hot tubs wove their way around the thick black-green vines of ivy. A few tangles of legs hung over the sides of the hammocks strung low between the locust trees.

"That woman is naked," Stephen said in an unintentionally high-pitched voice.

"Yeah, Angel does that sometimes. Sorry, guess I should have warned you. Don't worry, she's very nice, and mostly, she wears clothes. She must have been in the hot tub," Drew said.

"Okay, but I'm not shaking hands."

"No problem. Of course, if I had that body, I'd go naked in the grocery store. "

"Your body is every bit as nice as hers," Stephen said.

"Okay, that was weird. Don't say that again."

"Actually, Drew, I often go naked in the grocery store, those butch girls in produce love it." Angel reached out and captured Drew in a full body hug. "Honey, you look wonderful. But no Maggie? I know you're here on business, but no Maggie? I'm so disappointed. How is that girl, still making something extraordinary out of the mundane?"

"Oh, yes, Maggie's fine. Same as always. You look great. I like the new hair. Sorry, this is Stephen Shaunessey. This is Angel, our hostess."

"Nice to meet you, welcome to Angel's, heaven on earth to women of all genders and an occasional biological male or two. And this is Magna, Marta, and Mona." Angel put her arms around the three young women who surrounded her. "They're at your service. If you get confused, just call them M&Ms. That's their stage name. Okay, the girls will help you upstairs. I assume you want to get settled and get over to the bank. I know I promised I wouldn't ask any questions about that, but if you have any good gossip, I know you'll throw it my way first."

Drew and Stephen left the suitcases and M&Ms in Angel's

private condo. "I wonder which one is the green M&M," Stephen said, letting out a low whistle as he and Drew crossed over Bradford Street and headed for Commercial.

"I know. That Angel, you gotta love a woman who lives that kind of life. Okay, now you promised. Make nice with the locals. Looks like we start with him," Drew said as they were stopped by the crowd gathered in front of the yellow vinyl police tape. They made their way carefully to the front and were met by the outstretched hands of a police officer who looked to be about two years out of high school. They showed their IDs, assured him they were not carrying any weapons, slipped under the tape, and asked to be escorted to the bank. He seemed confused and impressed, and after radioing someone named Sergeant Jensen, he walked them down Commercial Street the six blocks to the bank.

The small red brick bank was ringed with police officers standing around in clumps of two or three. They had on various color uniforms indicating different departments. Two large fire trucks, lights flashing, were parked one behind the other in the middle of the street in front of the bank. The air carried the sour smell of something rotting even at this distance. The young officer, who had escorted them, steered them to the front of the bank toward a large beefy Italian-looking man whose large arms were fighting for more room inside the sleeves of his white cotton shirt. She read the name on his gold badge.

"Chief Santora, I'm Drew Morgan, this is Stephen Shaunessey. We spoke earlier today. A pleasure to meet you, and we hope the task force can be of help to you. What can you tell us so far?" Drew extended her hand.

"I'm glad you're here. God, what an awful day. It goes this way. We got one of your bank robbers you been looking for. At least that's how it looks to us. Bank opened at seven, only two tellers for Saturday and the assistant manager, but he was in the office. Four people waiting in line inside, a couple of others out here waiting to use the cash machine. All of a sudden, the door busts open and a woman runs in, there's barking, a dog runs in right after, she pulls out a gun, starts yelling, and Billy Baychamp shoots 'em both. Kills 'em both."

"Who's Mr. Baychamp? And where is he now?" Drew asked.

"He's one of my people. Been workin' the bank as a side job about a month now. We talked to him, took his weapon, and sent him home to his wife. He was pretty shook up."

"Okay, I assume you're still canvassing."

"Yes, lotta folks around here this morning. That's gonna take awhile. Your people from New York are inside. Been here awhile, I'm thinkin' they'll be done soon. Everything in there's just like it was. 'Cept for the woman, of course, she got taken to the med center, but she was dead 'bout the time they put her in the ambulance. They kept her there. Dr. Austin's there now doing the autopsy, I guess."

"And the people in the bank? Where are they now?" Drew asked.

"We took preliminary statements and took them down to my office. I think they were taking them to get fed about now." Captain Santora looked at his watch. "But they'll take 'em back over there when they're done. I think I'm gonna head back over there now myself. Just let my folks know when you're done and they'll show you the way."

"We will. Thanks very much."

The inside of the bank was small, no bigger than an average living room. There was a raised white marble counter to the left with two teller stations. On the right was a four-foot-high white wooden rail, behind which sat a cherry finish desk with a computer. A small burgundy velvet chair sat empty facing the desk. Two heavy glass and gold gild chandeliers hung from the high ceiling. In the middle of the white stone floor lay a very large, very bloody full grown dead German shepherd.

A pool of thick and drying blood circled the dog in a span of about a foot, in some places two feet. There were smears of blood next to the dog and one other larger pool of blood where the body of the woman had obviously been removed. A few partial shoe tracks could be seen around the farthest edges of that pool. Small ribbons of blood ran almost the length of the room and the white railing had a faint splatter of blood at least halfway up. The two evidence technicians were standing in back of the teller counter, hunched over, writing and tagging evidence bags.

"Jesus, this is so final scene in '*Carrie*,'" Stephen said.

They were standing just outside the circle of blood, bending forward over the dog, its eyes fixed in a permanent sad gaze.

"Look at that." Drew pointed to the area just below the dog's front shoulder. The area was matted down in a line about four inches wide all the way down to the middle of its belly. "Hmm, the dog got shot first. She fell on top. Don't ya think?"

"I don't know. Why do you say that?"

"Well look, the matted part, it comes all the way around to the belly. If she had fallen on her back and her arm had just fallen over the dog, only the top would be matted. So the dog had to fall first and her on top or on the side with her arm hanging over. How the hell did the dog get shot? What the hell is the dog even doing here?"

"Geez. This is going to be me someday. Die hugging a dead dog. What kind of karma did this woman have anyway?" Stephen stretched his lower back. "Okay, what else? I'm getting hungry."

"Hungry? You're a sick man. All right, I need to talk to the techs. And remember we agreed, I do the talking this time and you just take notes."

"Yeah, whatever. That Stan Raspberry guy from New York is a total homophobe."

"Like I said, you take notes. Just make sure I don't forget anything."

"Yeah, like that would ever happen."

Stan Raspberry and Jake Whinman were just logging their last two bags of evidence. "Stan, Jake, nice to see you again, if that's the right thing to say," Drew said, extending her hand.

"Yes, well, this is a wrap. Here's what we have," Raspberry said, passing on the handshake. "The bank has no video, so there's nothing that will help us there. We took pictures from every angle. Here's the cop's gun, standard issue .45 with all rounds discharged. We got blood samples from every position. No bullets recovered from inside, so this guy must have been some great shot. We think at least two of the bullets are in the dog. I suppose the coroner can fill you in on how many are in the suspect. Here's the suspect's weapon, or so we're told."

"What's that mean, Detective? Or so you're told?" Stephen said.

"Look at it. You decide." Raspberry shoved a small handgun encased in plastic across the counter.

"A .22? Who the hell robs a bank with a .22-caliber handgun?" Drew said.

"Exactly what we thought. In any event, it's no match to the weapons used in the robberies in New York." Raspberry looked down and began flipping the pages in his spiral notebook.

"Yes, no match for Boston, either," Drew said, fingering the gun. "Where did you find the weapon?"

"More to the point, why did you move it before we got here?" Stephen said.

"I don't like your attitude or your accusation." Raspberry spat the words at Stephen.

"Okay, okay, time-out. Where did you find the weapon, Detective?" Drew took a step forward to move between Raspberry and Stephen.

"This is why we needed federal agents from D.C. on this case," Stephen said in a raised voice over Drew's shoulder.

"I know what you need, pal," Raspberry said, sticking his thumbs in his belt and hiking his pants hard.

"You keep Krispy Kreme doughnuts in your pants, Raspberry?" Stephen said.

"Enough. I said enough. Stop right now. Let's try it this way. Detective Whinman?"

"Chief Santora gave it to us when we got here. That's why it's in a baggie inside our evidence bag. You did notice it was double bagged right?" Whinman looked down at the weapon.

"What? They moved the gun before you got here? That's outrageous."

"Yep, it sure is. He said it came from over there," Whinman pointed to a spot just below the blood spatter along the railed

11

portion of the interior. "All we could do was bag it and take a lot of pictures of the place they said they found it."

"Okay, show me exactly." Drew moved toward the spot on the other side of the bank. Whinman moved with her.

"He said it was right here, pointing toward the railing and away from the body. He said the barrel was so close it was almost touching the railing. No blood on it, though. Not to the naked eye anyway. Of course we'll test it with fluorescent powder after we check it for prints."

"Did he say why he moved it?" Drew asked, still staring at the floor.

"No, not really. Seemed kind of excited about it, though. Thought I would leave the rest of that part of it to you all. I'm just a soldier, bag and tag. I'll leave the politickin' to you. "

"That's fair. Can you get the digital camera back out for me please?"

"Ah, yep." Whinman walked back to the other side of the bank where Raspberry and Stephen were standing back to back in a brief detente. He took the camera out without a word to either and walked back over to where Drew was now standing next to the dog.

"Here's what I need you to do. Shoot every inch from here to the railing. And can you use two disks please, one for you and one for me? I'd like to look at these today." Drew mapped the route in the air with her finger.

"Ah, every inch of what exactly?"

"I'm sorry. The floor, detective. Every inch of the floor in about a four-foot width. From here to there." Drew said, still pointing. "Can you do that for me?"

"Yep. Take about forty minutes for two disks." Whinman adjusted the camera.

"Okay, thank you. Could you send someone to deliver it to Angel's on Bradford, as well as copies of your evidence notebooks? We're going to get some quick breakfast, then do the witness interviews."

"Yep, my notebook's on the counter." Whinman was on his knees, adjusting the lens on the camera, snapping pictures.

Chapter Two

The late morning sky was throwing patches of blue gray light in oblong squares along the weathered boards of McMillan Wharf. The sour smell from the small fleet of fishing boats became stronger as Drew and Stephen approached Bongo's Diner at the end of the pier. The waitress, a local drag queen whose name tag read "Carlotta Tendant", seated Drew and Stephen in the back booth and assured them she would rush their order as she skated on Rollerblades toward the kitchen.

"I'll tell ya, so far it doesn't look like this is one of our girls," Drew said.

"Yeah, I don't think so, either. The M.O. is totally different here. I don't see it. What was with the pictures of the floor you asked Barney Fife for at the end there?" Stephen absentmindedly began sketching out the crime scene with a blue crayon on the white paper table cloth.

"I don't know yet. Let's see what they show or don't show. Let's just eat and get on to the interviews. Okay, so now who was the blond who answered your phone this morning?"

"How do you know he was blond?"

"Because they're always blond. Your sex life is George Michael from the seventies to the nineties inclusive."

"Oh, that's nice, very nice. Here we go. It's lesbian lecture time."

"No, not here we go. I just think you could be a little more

13

selective, that's all." Drew began marking over elements of the crime scene sketch with a black flair.

"If I had sex as often as you do, my balls would be the size of Montana."

"There's something I wanted to think about over breakfast."

"You started it."

"You're such a romantic."

"Romantic schmomantic. I think you know me better than that by now."

"Fine, I'm just saying..."

"Drew, darling, my best friend in the whole world, don't take this wrong, but you have been a royal pain in my ass since the day Maggie left, and frankly, I don't take this much grief from someone I'm not sleeping with."

"This conversation is not about Maggie."

"Oh, silly me. What was I thinking? Of course not. This conversation isn't about Maggie. How could this conversation possibly be about Maggie? How could any conversation be about Maggie? God forbid we should actually fucking talk about Maggie. Much better you should just take out all your displaced anger on your friends."

Drew stared silently. "Listen, Stephen."

"No, you listen. Maggie's been gone for six months. Six months, Drew, and you don't even want to talk about it. You don't want to talk to anybody. You don't want to see anybody. You don't want to go anywhere. You can't keep isolating yourself like this, it's not healthy. I'm telling you if you don't start dealing with some of those issues and all your displaced anger, you're never going to start healing and..."

"Oh, good. Are we going to do the entire breakfast conversation in lesbian therapy speak? You know how I just love that."

"You're impossible." Stephen pointed his fork at Drew.

"You talk too much." Drew pointed her fork at Stephen.

"You don't talk at all."

"You think you can run everyone's life."

"You've forgotten what it's like to have a life."

"You're such an asshole." Drew put her fork down and broke

into a small smile.

"You're such an idiot." Stephen began to laugh.

"I love you, Shaunessey."

"I love you, too, Morgan."

"Good, next time let's argue about something more interesting. Now let's eat." Drew lightly salted her barely cooked over-easy eggs and stirred a small amount of cream into her coffee. "So you said you talked to your mom. Is that right? How is she?"

"Still mourning the loss of Mussolini."

"So the same then. Okay, really, who were you with last night? Anybody I know?"

"William." Stephen looked away.

"William? Please tell me it was William Six and not William Seven."

"Guilty, I'm afraid."

"Good god. I thought he transferred to U.C. Berkeley. Or was that William Six? I can't remember now. It's like you're running some personal catch-and-release program for Williams."

"Actually, I think all but William One are in California now. So that would be a yes to both. Are you going to eat those potatoes?"

"No, here." Drew slid the plate across the table. "See now, I liked William One."

"Of course you did. He had more estrogen than you do."

"What's wrong with that? I loved shopping with him, it was great cardio. I'll play because it's the last fun I will get to have today. What was Tyrannosaurus Ex doing back in town?"

"Funny. He's not, he was just in for the weekend, her mom is sick."

"Hard to keep those pronouns straight, isn't it? I'm sorry to hear that. Are you going to eat those potatoes or what? We need to go."

"My impeccably toned Irish ass you're sorry. And I'm not eating these; they're too greasy, even for me." Stephen folded his napkin over the plate.

"Oh, look who's suddenly picky about what he puts in his mouth." Drew threw a twenty on the table.

"And on that note, we have witnesses waiting."

Chapter Three

The building housing the police department was a two-story white clapboard structure in the center of town. It was surrounded on all sides by sculptured gardens. The contrast of winter white and lush green made the building look and feel more Southern than New England. Drew and Stephen walked in the side door and made their way up two flights of stairs. They found Chief Santora who led them to the door of a large conference room that was being guarded by two uniformed officers.

"We kept all the witnesses together, but they haven't talked to each other at all about what happened, so you should get clean interviews. I assume my people can be in here, too," Santora said, his hand on the doorknob.

"Sure, Chief, that's fine. I assumed you would want your own folks to sit in on the interviews. It is your jurisdiction," Drew said.

"Okay, good. Officers Lambert and Rumpe will sit in. One more thing before you go in. Remember it was supposed to be Carnival today. That's a big deal around here, so some of these folks got dressed already this morning."

"That's fine," Drew said.

"Just thought you should know." Santora threw open the door.

The conference room was enormous. Its fourteen-foot-high windows were draped with aging blue velvet curtains held back by ornate brass bows the size of punch bowls. The walls were either painted or had evolved into a faint gray. A nine-inch mahogany chair rail ran the length of all four walls, and against the farthest wall ran an ornately carved mahogany bench covered by a well-worn blue velvet cushion. The room held six people.

The first was a young Hispanic man, maybe Cuban, about twenty-two, maybe younger, dressed in a bright blue halter top, a tropical flowered skirt tied at the left hip, five-inch turquoise heels, and a three-foot-tall headdress made up of troll dolls of different sizes. Some of the dolls were dressed in bikinis, some in miniature tropical flowered shirts. Some sat atop tiny ladders, some in tiny convertible cars, some were posed in sexual positions and two near the bottom were playing underneath a tiny waterfall with real running water. He was leaning against a hand-painted sign that read, "My Name is Mango, ten dollars to see my Pango."

At the far end of the bench half-sitting, half-standing were two young men. One was about six-foot-two, although it was hard to tell his exact height because he was standing inside of a giant foam rubber red and white-striped popcorn box. The only visible signs that the box housed a human were his feet, which were covered in red and white-striped socks and old-fashioned red high-top sneakers, and his face from the nose up, which was mostly obscured by a bright yellow crepe paper wig. Next to him was a much shorter man shouldering a car-sized Cracker Jack box. His head was covered with basketball-sized pieces of foam caramel corn. A large piece of the box from his waist to just above his knees was cut out, and that part of his body was sealed inside a plain white wrapper that had the word "Prize" stenciled across it in light blue block letters. From their body language, it was clear that he and Popcorn had come together.

At the opposite end of the room, looking out the window, was a man about thirty-five dressed in a Chanel knock-off pale pink suit with covered buttons, five-inch pink platform shoes, a sculpted blond wig that flipped up perfectly at the shoulders—like a blond "That Girl" on steroids—and a hat that was covered in a variety of plastic pharmaceuticals from aspirin to Vicodin that had been glued in neat rows over every inch. High on the left shoulder was a small spatter of what Drew knew, even at that distance, was blood. He held a pink vinyl purse with a button affixed that read "Prozac Barbie."

At the farthest end of the bench, a middle-aged couple sat side by side heads down with their eyes closed. The man was in his mid-sixties and dressed in a green plaid collared shirt, a white belt, sea green Sansabelt slacks and white shoes. A form of heterosexual dress known affectionately in the gay community as the "full Cleveland." The woman was a little younger but looked more weathered. She wore a black T-shirt, black walking shorts, black knee socks, and black tennis shoes.

"Jesus, Mary, and Joseph." Drew sighed under her breath. "Hello, everyone, my name is Drew Morgan, and this is my partner, Stephen Shaunessey. We're prosecutors from Washington, D.C. We'd like to thank you for waiting so long for us to get down here. I'm sure you're all anxious to get out of here as quickly as you can. We know you've all had a terrible experience this morning, but I'm sure you can understand that we need to interview each of you about what you saw and heard before we can get you out of here. I think to speed things up a bit, we'll talk to you two at a time. Officers Lambert and Rumpe will be working with us, as well. We'll start with the two of you, if you don't mind." Drew pointed to Mango and Barbie.

The anteroom off the conference room was small, with only a small leather top table and wooden mahogany chairs. The walls were covered floor to ceiling with a deep red flowered raised velvet wallpaper, giving the impression that they were sitting inside a 1940s steamer trunk. The two police officers shuffled the chairs aside and leaned against the back wall, thumbs in their gun belts. Mango and Barbie took chairs across the table from each other.

"Let's start with names," Stephen said.

"I'm John Robert Flynn the third," Barbie said in a deep baritone.

"Oh, goodie, there are two more of you," Mango said.

"Bite me, fruit boy."

"I would but...caps." Mango tapped his front tooth with the two-inch nail of his left index finger. "They can't cut through plastic."

"Ah, wit, from the people who brought you Pearl Harbor." Barbie turned his back and crossed his legs gently at the knee.

"Can I just get the names, girls and boys, so we can all move on?" Stephen tapped his pencil sharply on the table.

"I'm Cuban and Japanese." Mango shook his head hard to the right, inadvertently flinging the lime green Incredible Hulk troll doll off the fringe of his hat directly at Stephen. He caught it mid-flight.

"Okay then." Stephen held the doll in his right hand. "Like I said. Name?"

"Mango."

"Okay, Mango, here's what you need to know about me. I'm a forty-year-old federal prosecutor. What that means for you is I don't do cute."

"Alex Rodriguez."

"There you go. Now what happened at the bank?"

Their stories were essentially the same. They had gone to the bank separately, each to deposit the proceeds from their performances from the night before. Barbie was the last in line and Mango was standing in front of her. They each described hearing a loud barking noise, then the glass door to the bank banging open and the suspect running in chased by a dog. At that point, their stories differed.

"I didn't even duck really, there wasn't time. As soon as I turned around, bang he shot her, then bang, bang, he shot the dog, and that's how this happened." Barbie ran her hand lightly over the now dried blood splatter on her left shoulder. "Then I started screaming and noticed Bongo here cowering on the floor at my feet."

"Mango."

"Mongrel. There was more than one dog in that bank." Barbie tilted her head slightly to the right. Her wig and hat failed to follow.

"You crazy, too. It not happen that way at all. She come in screaming, then bang, bang, he shoot the dog, then bang, bang, he shoot her. He tell us to get down, then I fall to the floor. You think you so brave, you no brave, that skirt too tight for you to move." Mango looked over his left shoulder at the two police officers still leaning against the back wall, then leaned forward and whispered loudly, "That cop in there, he crazy. I thought he shoot everybody."

Ultimately, they could not agree on the exact sequence of events, particularly when it came to the shooting. Drew and Stephen knew it was not at all unusual for witnesses to have widely differing accounts, even if they were standing side by side during the event. Trauma often altered time lines and identifications. They were hoping the rest of the witnesses would help to even out the story.

The older couple, Bill and Loretta Butler, were from Memphis.

"We just like to go to interesting places is all, so we came here this year. And it sure is interesting. We sure didn't think nothin' like this would happen, though. No, sir, we sure did not." Loretta Butler ran her puffy fingers across the table as if she were playing a piano only she could see. "Startin' to think maybe God gave me an interestin' enough life just taking care o' the King's house. Maybe that's just enough for us."

"What? King who?" Drew said.

"You must be kiddin' me now," Loretta raised both hands to her mouth. "What king? That's a good one."

Drew looked in puzzlement at Stephen and shrugged her shoulders.

"I think she means Elvis." Stephen smiled broadly.

"Oh, you love Elvis, too?" Loretta said.

"Well, love might be overstating it, but I certainly know who he is, or was," Stephen said. "That's really interesting, Mrs. Butler, but for now, maybe we could concentrate on what happened at the bank."

"Better Bill should tell it, he saw more'n I did." Loretta resumed playing the air piano.

"Okay then, Mr. Butler?"

"It started out real normal. We was just waiting in line trying to cash some travelers checks for the trip home. Hope this don't make us late goin' back or I lose a day's pay. Only get two weeks. Used one in Branson, then one here. Hate to lose a day's pay. I make ice cream cones. Flat bottom cake. Not those waffle kind they got here. Flat bottom cake. Make the batter, pour it into the molds, boil for eight minutes. Everybody thinks you bake 'em, but you don't, no, sir, you boil 'em. People don't know that. They think it's interesting."

"That's great, but if we could just get on to what happened at the bank," Stephen said.

"I'm tellin' ya what happened at the bank. I'm sayin' that people think it's interesting. How you make ice cream cones, especially the boilin' 'em part. So that's what I was tellin' those two girls in back of us. You know, those guy girls, the one of 'em dressed like Barbie and that other, ya know the fruit guy."

"Now, Bill, don't go sayin' things like that. It ain't polite," Loretta said.

"I don't mean fruit like that way. I'm sayin' his name was a fruity-like name. Like pineapple or whatever it was," Bill said.

"Mango?" Stephen said.

"Right, Mango," Bill said, snapping his fingers. "See, Loretta, fruit like in that way."

"Sorry now, I didn't mean to get on ya like that. But sometimes you do say stuff not quite how ya mean it, then people get a bad impression. Mango, yes, that sure is a fruity name."

"Okay, Mr. Butler. So you were at the bank standing in line in front of Barbie and Mango, telling them about your work, then what happened?" Drew said.

"It was the damndest thing ya ever saw. Door flew open so hard I 'bout thought it was gonna come right off the hinges. Woman runs in screaming and cursin' a blue streak, some dog with her barkin', she's kickin' it, then she just starts screamin' 'Money, money.' Next thing I know, I hear a gun goin' off. Ain't heard that sound since Nam. Didn't never want to hear it again, neither. So, shit, I just grabbed Loretta and put her down and got on top of her and stayed there till the shootin' stopped. Whole damn thing didn't take no more than a couple of minutes far as I can tell. That cop was shakin' like a new recruit by the time we got up. Pretty clear to me he never shot nobody before. Shot a woman and a dog, too. Damndest thing I ever saw, I tell ya."

Stephen thought the "Money, money" part of the story sounded suspect, and he knew Drew would not let it go unchecked. It was just a matter of time before the real story would be drawn out. Stephen loved to watch Drew work witnesses. Totally in control, weaving in and out. Seamless. Her green eyes at once intimidating and charming, half savior, half jewel thief.

Click, click click, it was the sound of Drew's pen on the desk, and those eyes in just this light, the green of new summer apples, that drew him back into memory, like a magnet to metal.

Thump, thump, thump. Stephen and three young Italian boys bounced the large red rubber ball back and forth and across in the faded blue four-square box in the playground of their lower-middle-class Catholic grade school. Gently at first, back, forth, across, then picking up speed until the biggest one, Tony Masarelli, picked it up and heaved the ball full force into Stephen's face. Then it began in earnest. Stephen found himself face-down as usual, hands covering his face, while the other boys threw fists into his back and small, thin arms. If asked, Stephen would have said he preferred the beatings of the Irish boys; it was more familiar and easier. With them, once they drew a little blood, they were satisfied and moved on to the next weak link in the chain. The Italians were much worse. First, they would draw a crowd, then the taunting would begin, humiliation a key element. Not just a quick punch in the nose or a few glancing blows off the body, but both and more. They fought with the full fury of being nine.

Then, *click, click, click, click, click.* The sound of Sister Angelica's steel heel guards, children scattering, the feel of the sweet, impossibly old Sister Angelica scooping him up off the steaming asphalt. She would lead him to the boy's bathroom, tilt his head back, and stick giant wads of Kleenex up his tiny nose until they stuck out like fat straws. Then she would remove her freshly laundered white handkerchief from its secret hiding place in her left sleeve and begin dabbing at the blood still mapping its way down the collar of his over-starched white shirt. The blood

23

would run red to pink but no farther.

She would walk him down the long corridor to the fifth-grade classroom and plop him down in her desk chair. The classroom was still empty. By now, the rest of the boys were in Father Mike's catechism class. No doubt taking copious notes on the whole redemption angle. Sister would start her well-worn lecture about turning the other cheek and how bullies only feel brave when the forest is empty.

The lecture would hum in his head as he looked around the classroom. Past the pictures of the sacred heart and the sixteen neatly spaced variations of the crucifixion until his gaze fixed on the thick frosted glass of the top half of the classroom door. He was looking hard, waiting for it. And just as it always had, a bobbing shadow appeared on the other side and through a tiny chip in the lower left corner, a small startling flash of green appeared and just as quickly was gone.

Although he never told Sister, Stephen was convinced that the recurring vision in green was his guardian angel. And even though he always wondered why his guardian angel could not appear just a tad earlier, say, before he ended up face-down on the playground, its appearance gave him a deep sense of peace. When she finished the lecture, Sister Angelica would reach deep into her top desk drawer, fish out a Hershey bar, unwrap the top half, and hand it to him as if he were still a small boy. She would run her hands in soothing circles around his shoulder blades and reach over and gently slide a holy card of St. Francis into his shirt pocket as he rocked gently back and forth, turning the chocolate over on his tongue, coating his teeth with sugar.

It wasn't until the next year that Stephen was told that it had been Drew, and not Sister Angelica's finely tuned sense of timing, that had saved him all those early-summer days. Jimmy Pastora told him one day after band practice. Not in a kind way, but in a taunting way as if Stephen had needed something as pathetic as a girl to save him.

It was in the heat of the moment. Jimmy Pastora was really mad that Stephen had just beaten him out as first chair saxophone. Jimmy didn't have that much going for him. He had been accidentally dropped onto the white marble baptismal fountain by his uncle during his baptism, with a wicked result. A large singular black scar dotted with smaller black scars ran the entire length of the left side of his skull. No amount of hair rearranging could hide it. Whatever else would become of Jimmy Pastora, in some measure, he would always be the boy who appeared to have a highway running through his head.

Stephen was embarrassed at first, in part, that a girl had played some role in his survival of fifth grade, but more because he had actually fallen for all that guardian angel mess. For that year and the next, he and Drew cautiously edged their way toward a friendship. In her, Stephen found relief. Her passion for all things boy-like—sports, climbing trees, throwing rocks at the street lamps—somehow allowed him to take a break from the burdens of his gender.

They became inseparable until seventh grade when Stephen's parents parted ways with the Catholic Church over birth control and they sent Stephen off to pubic school. The Catholics and the publics didn't mix, and Stephen didn't see her again until law school.

The reconnection was not instantaneous. They had been excited at first, when each realized that the other was attending the same school, but their lunch the first week proved awkward. Life had produced in each of them new corners and edges. The pieces no longer fit together so easily. They cautiously circled each other for six months. It wasn't until the tryouts for the school's mock trial competition, which pitted trial teams from different schools against one another in the re-creation of a famous trial, that their old attachment drew them together like co-conspirators.

Everyone had to pick a partner to act as his or her co-counsel for tryouts. Stephen picked Drew for two reasons. First, because he knew that she had what he himself would never have—the killer instinct. The power to draw a witness in, charm, disarm, then unblinkingly pull the trigger. Second, because she was the only person he knew who carried a copy of the Constitution in her wallet because "you just never know." Behavior he found extremely odd and strangely arousing.

It never occurred to Drew or Stephen, until the day of tryouts, that out of sixty students, Drew would prove to be the only woman in the entire competition. They were called to try out last. Twenty minutes before they were called in, they were handed a brief summary of a famous case and a rough outline of the testimony the key witness would offer. Stephen was assigned to develop the decidedly less glamorous, but no less important, direct examination and Drew would handle the cross. They had no way of knowing then that that random decision would form the footprint of their entire professional relationship. In that moment, their singular goal was to win.

And they did, or rather, Drew did. Stephen liked to tell himself later that Drew made first chair on the team only because Stephen had deliberately set the witness up on direct to be vulnerable on cross on several key points. Of course it was a lie. Or maybe it wasn't. Maybe he had done just that. The point was, it didn't matter.

Whatever Stephen had or hadn't done on direct was lost the moment Drew spoke. She didn't even rise from her seat, asking the first three questions while still seated at counsel table. A technique that relaxed the witness, made Drew seem friendly, less combative than the others who had tested her story earlier in the day. In the few brief minutes that followed, Drew made five or six perfectly calculated verbal incisions in the witness's story. Not a stray bullet in the round. With less than ten questions, Drew had completely dismantled the plaintiff's case. Word spread pretty quickly the next day that Professor Samuelson had picked the first "girl" to be on the team. Stephen made the team through the back door.

He was third chair, backdrop, the legal equivalent of an understudy. Relegated to researching and briefing some of the legal issues that would be argued during the trial. Regardless, he was still expected to be at every practice run-through and began spending deliberately more time than was required with Drew and Joe Hogan, second chair, discussing strategy.

Joe Hogan figured out pretty quickly how little interest he had in spending more time than necessary with people he had no chance of ever sleeping with. He began a slow retreat from the long coffeed strategy sessions, and eventually they saw him only at run-throughs. With him gone, the strategy sessions moved from the student union to Stephen's off-campus apartment. More precisely, off-campus bedroom. A very small studio containing a stained yellow pull-out sofa, a blue and white-striped lawn chair, and a coffeepot.

The absence of a desk or table to work at was more a product of poverty than seduction plan on Stephen's part, but it did work out nicely most of the time. They sat for hours on that sofa, Stephen able to break Drew's concentration only long enough to refill her coffee cup.

Drew would talk endlessly about new cases to research, a new avenue to explore, a better approach. And Stephen would listen and listen, then stop listening and look. Into those eyes, those amazing eyes, those always-in-motion, darting, drink-everything-in, leave-nothing-to-chance eyes searching for a signal, any signal. *Was that a smile? Did she leave her hand on the book on my lap just long enough for it to be a sign? Can I really be attracted to a woman in this way? Could I be so lucky that she is really bisexual? Is this more than the late maturing of a schoolboy crush? She never talks about seeing anyone. Does she ever talk about anything but the law? Is she waiting for me to make the first move?*

After about a month of couch torture, Drew finally spoke of something other than the law. Stopping on her way out the door, she said, "Hey, I'm having a small get-together tomorrow night. Some friends of mine are coming into town for the weekend. Why don't you come by and meet them? Around seven thirty?"

Stephen could manage only, "Uh, sure, okay."

Stephen spent the next day alternating between trying on his clothes and rerunning that moment in his mind and on the phone with his friends. Prying apart and rearranging every syllable trying to break whatever code might have been contained in it. Having exhausted his friends' patience with the "can I feel this way about a woman" monologue, he dressed in his tightest Levi's 501s with the ripped thigh, a white Oxford shirt, black belt, and Doc Marten's, so new to fashion then that they were still referred to as Doctor Marten's, and on the fact that he would know the true meaning of the invitation soon enough.

He was relieved that it took a couple of minutes before the buzzer for the outer door of the apartment building sounded his entrance. Breathing time. The door to the apartment was slightly open, and the faintest rumble of a party made its way into the hall. A few steps into the apartment, a woman Stephen did not know came over.

"Hi, I'm Billy."

"Hi, Stephen, I'm a friend of Drew's."

"Oh, right, Steve, from the law thing, right?"

"It's Stephen. And, yes, the mock trial team."

"Oh, yeah, right. Sorry, I don't know too much about that law stuff myself, I work for UPS. Anyway, come on in. We're just hanging out. Beer's in the kitchen. And Drew is, I dunno, somewhere in there." She pointed in a sweeping motion toward the back of the apartment.

As he moved toward the back, Stephen surveyed the room. The rows of packed bookshelves and expensively framed artwork were lost on him. He directed his attention to an immediate headcount of the participants. If there were no strays in the back, there was an even twelve. Bingo, no singles, clearly all couples. With that confidence, he turned the corner into the kitchen.

Drew had her back to the door, bent over the tap on the keg, apparently straining to make some adjustment.

"Hey, here you are. I mean, hi." Stephen instinctively put his hands in his pockets, suddenly uncomfortable. "Great apartment."

Drew glanced over her shoulder just long enough to place the voice with a face. "Hey, hi, sorry, I'm trying to get this damn thing to pump a little quicker. Can you hand me that knife?"

"Sure." Stephen slid the knife up across the back of Drew's shoulder. "Need some help?" he said as he slid his front as close to Drew's back as he could without actually touching.

"Honey, I told you to get the bigger tap. This happens every time. You spend half the party in here trying to pry beer out of that thing. Here let me try, and give me that knife. I don't want a rerun of the emergency room visit of last year. We can't afford it. Excuse me, oh, by the way, I'm Maggie," said the voice that came out of the body that had just come out of the bedroom as it slid its hands around Stephen's waist and gently moved him aside.

"Oh, sorry, Stephen, this is my lover Maggie. Maggie, Stephen. Remember, I told you, the guy from back home who's on the team with me."

"Oh, right, the man who has commanded so much of my girl's attention these past few weeks. Nice to finally meet you, and, hey, nice jeans," Maggie said, turning her attention back to the tap.

Stephen grabbed an empty cup from the counter, turned to the sink, and began running his fingers under the spit of water. "Nice to meet you, too."

"Honey, I think we can do a little better than water for your friend. Why don't you get Stephen a beer out of the fridge? Our friends always bring us a backup supply. They know us so well."

"Oh, sorry sure, here," Drew opened the refrigerator door and handed Stephen a Corona. "That okay?"

"Uh, sure, yeah great, I love Corona. I just hardly ever drink it because it's out of my price range." Stephen took an excessively long swig.

"Ours too, but luckily, our friends actually have real jobs." Maggie turned back from the keg and wiped her hands on the thighs of her jeans, staining them slightly with dribbles of beer. "Come on, I'll introduce you to the working class." Maggie slipped her arm across the top of Stephen's shoulders and steered him toward the living room.

After spending as much time as possible scanning the name of every cassette tape and book on the shelves, Stephen finally settled himself in a chair in the farthest corner of the room. Drew's friends were nice enough, but they had all obviously known each other for a very long time and spent most of the night recounting that history with one another. This suited him perfectly. He wasn't in a talking mood now anyway and was just as content to watch. Less opportunity to say or do the wrong thing. Give away his original and, what now seemed utterly absurd, intentions. The most disappointing part of this very disappointing evening was that he couldn't work up even the slightest dislike for Maggie.

The attraction was obvious. Maggie was almost unapproachably beautiful. A head full of hair the color of brick, body slim and firm. She was sweet and warm and had made, it seemed, good choices in friends. She seemed the right counterbalance for Drew. Drew got to have the energy and Maggie got to absorb it.

After the second hour of watching Drew and Maggie, mostly Drew, as they chatted and patted in earnest with their friends, Stephen got up, walked toward the kitchen with his empty beer bottle, ready to make his escape. Someone knocked on the door, a couple late in arriving. As Stephen rounded the door of the kitchen, the rest of the partygoers rose to give the new arrivals a warm round of hugs. Stephen tossed the bottle, then stopped one last time in the doorway, slipping in one last brief look at Drew in her element, one last sigh to lost possibility.

"You must be awfully disappointed. I'm sorry you didn't have a better time. I hope you'll come back." Maggie was standing in the doorway of the bedroom. Stephen turned toward her voice.

"What? Oh, no, not at all. It was a great party. It's just that it's so late. I think I better go."

"It's ten thirty. And I'm not talking about the party. I'm talking about me."

"You? What? I don't understand."

"Yes, you do. She didn't mention me. You came here expecting something, or hoping for something—which didn't include me."

"No, I didn't."

"Yes, you did," Maggie said, breaking into a broad smile.

"No, I didn't, really. Drew didn't tell me about you, or maybe she did and I just don't remember. Anyway, listen, there's nothing going on. All that time we spend together, we really are working on the case. Really. We really are. I'm gay anyway. Well, bi. Well, really gay. Okay, that sounds stupid. Anyway, I need to go."

"Stephen, relax. I have no doubts about Drew. This isn't the first time, you know. If it makes you feel any better, it happens quite often. She's intense, smart, funny, edgy. I'm sure you gave her clues, and I'm equally sure she didn't get it. It happens. Who wouldn't want to explore all the options? The thing is, we've been together so long, she's just not plugged into that energy anymore. Never was really. I practically had to hit her over the head to get her to notice I wanted to be more than her lab partner. Sorry." Maggie slid next to Stephen and wrapped her arm around his waist. "Please don't go. The good news is she makes an even better friend. Besides, you don't want those jeans to go totally to waste, and the two that just walked in are single. One boy, one girl. I'll let you decide."

Mr. Butler stuck to the story, and no matter how many times Drew asked him, he assured them that the suspect had yelled, "Money, money," before the shots rang out.

Popcorn and Cracker Jack were of little value. They were a couple from Cincinnati. Cracker Jack was using the ATM that was housed in a Plexiglas stall just outside the bank and Popcorn was standing right behind him half inside the stall, which was only big enough to hold one of them given their costumes. The Plexiglas must have muffled the sound of the suspect running past. They said they didn't hear anything until they heard gunshots, then screaming coming from inside the bank. At that point, Popcorn jumped forward into the ATM stall whereupon their respective popcorn balls became entangled and they had to be freed by two police officers.

Chapter Four

"What kind of cluster fuck of witnesses was that?" Drew said to Stephen, who was standing beside her in line at Grind, a coffee bar at the far east end of Commercial Street.

"Honestly. I feel like I'm standing at the intersection of the yellow brick road and Nathan Lane at midnight in the garden of good and evil." Stephen ordered a double espresso.

"And what is with those people from Memphis? Do you think she really cleans Elvis's house? Does she know he's still dead?" Drew ordered an iced half-caf half-decaf half-skim half-whole no whip latté with a dusting of cinnamon.

"High-maintenance woman latté with a sprinkle—grande," the barista barked to the young woman manning the espresso machine who was simultaneously steaming milk and having a heated discussion on her cellular headset with someone named "fucking asshole Bridget."

"I don't know what that Elvis thing was all about. I do know that either she saw more than she is saying in that bank this morning or she's as stupid as she looks." Stephen dumped two packets of Sweet'n Low in his tiny cup.

"I wouldn't even know where to place that bet. Come on, the doctor's waiting. I think the Doc in the Box is down about eight blocks to the left."

In the three hours that had passed since their arrival, Commercial Street had begun to come alive again. The bed and breakfasts of the east end were coughing out small groups of tourists, who snaked their way among the dozens of galleries in search of a way to pass an hour or two until the light afternoon drizzle passed. These were not the tourist traps like those sandwiched in between the taffy and T-shirt shops closer to the center of town. These were fine art galleries.

Maggie loved these galleries and this town. She often referred to it as her favorite place on Earth. It was the perfect blend of bohemia and serious art. Although Provincetown had begun as a Portuguese fishing and whaling port, a storm at the turn of the century had destroyed its wharves and fish packing houses. Rather than rebuild, Provincetown turned to the other great American industry—retail. Wealthy tourists from Boston and New York found the tip of Cape Cod an irresistible environment in which to build their large, seldom-used, summer homes. Along with the wealthy came the intellectual elite, including the most noted artists and writers of the early twentieth century. While the wealthy eventually grew tired of the long journey to the tip of the Cape, the art world had weighed anchor for good. Several well-known art schools were founded, as well as the country's first American theater company. The sixties brought well ... you know what the sixties brought. Once everyone's mind expanded, the gay people just slipped right in. And as with gay people everywhere, the cheer went up, "We're Here, We're Queer, Get Ralph Lauren's paint people on the phone, this place is a mess." The transformation from sleepy fishing village to gay mecca was complete by the mid-seventies.

It was the diversity and serious pursuit of art that drew Maggie to several summers of study at the Fine Arts Work Center. At first, she tried her best to get Drew to take a job in Boston instead of D.C. so she could study here year-round and commute by ferry to Boston on weekends. But Drew had failed to understand, at that point in their relationship, that Maggie's loving pursuit of photography was more than a very expensive hobby, and Drew's need for the excitement and the potential for a powerful role in Washington eventually won out.

Now, as Drew walked passed these galleries on this drizzly

blue-gray day, passing the rain-streaked windows filled with bleary black and white photos of seascapes tiptoeing toward the edge of winter and perfectly formed young men reclining in pouty dramatic pose, she pleaded quietly with herself for a chance to remake that decision.

Stephen instinctively patted her on the back. "She'll be back, you know she will, you two will be doin' it in the grave. You are still doin' it, right?"

Drew smiled sheepishly. "Shut up, you."

"She'll be back. And if she isn't, we still have plan B." Stephen stopped in front of a small gray cinder block building and checked the address. "Okay, this is it."

"Plan B?"

"Yes, plan B. That's where you and I get married and squeeze our eyes real tight twice a year and have sex." Three small bells on the door pinged as Stephen opened it.

"Good God. Okay, let's go see dead people."

The walls of the small outer office were covered with bright yellow wallpaper dotted with sunflowers. A very young, very attractive woman dressed in full leather and sporting what appeared to be at least twenty earrings in each ear, with the top half of a heart and arrow tattoo peeking over the top of her studded leather dog collar sat behind a low-rise green counter with a white picket fence painted across the front.

"Hi," Drew flashed her ID, "Drew Morgan and Stephen Shaunessey to see the doctor."

"Which one?"

"Oh, sorry. I'm Drew and this is Stephen."

"No kidding. Which doctor?"

"Oh, yes, sorry um, Dr. Austin."

"Okey dokey, back in a tic." The woman disappeared behind a swinging door.

"Look at you, Drew, all stammery in front of the young one."

"Was not. She just caught me by surprise is all. I didn't know there was more than one doctor in the whole town."

"I'll let you off the hook this time. But what do you think,

35

isn't this kind of odd for a doctor's office? What is she, like the Martha Stewart of doctors?"

"Actually, it came this way. Last year, it was a flower shop. We're big on alternate use of space here." A woman, who bore a striking resemblance to Demi Moore in the pottery wheel scene from *Ghost,* stood behind them, dressed in blue cotton shorts, a white T-shirt with the word "Womanship" emblazoned across it in black, all covered by a green lab jacket. "J.J. Austin," she said without extending a hand.

"Drew Morgan," Drew pointed to herself, "and Stephen Shaunessey. We're here to see the body and to discuss the autopsy, that is, if it's finished."

"Yes, heard all about you already. Small town, short wire, you know. This way, then."

Dr. Austin led them down a long narrow corridor that opened into a large room. At the far end of the room stood what clearly had been a florist's cooling unit. The front was composed of three floor-to-ceiling glass doors with heavy gauge steel handles. Inside, on a gurney lay the body of a woman covered to the chin with a white sheet.

"Here she is, then." Dr. Austin opened the nearest door and eased her way slowly inside. "Not much room in here, careful not to touch her."

"This is a first." Stephen held the door open for Drew to enter ahead of him.

"Best we could do. We don't hold bodies here, no need for autopsies. This is McMedicine, shoot and scoot. Coming in, then?" Dr. Austin said to Stephen.

"Actually, I don't think there's enough room, so I'll ... well ... watch through the door."

Drew squeezed as far down in the unit as possible, even though that required her to squeeze herself between the door and the doctor. The air itself seemed crowded, an odd mixture of medicine and mold overlaid with the faint smell of roses and lavender.

They stood for what seemed like more than a few seconds, casting minor sideways glances at each other. Drew caught herself and tried hard to force her eyes back to the body and struggled to no avail to put some inches of space between her and the doctor. After a tiny bit more shuffling, Dr. Austin removed the sheet. The woman was somewhere in her mid- to late fifties, about 5'8" with an average build. The most prominent features, of course, were the four distinct gunshot wounds to the upper torso. One at the top of the left arm, as if she had been shot from the side, one in the front of the left shoulder, and two more almost side by side in the middle of the chest. The body was otherwise unremarkable except for a deep red ring around the left wrist.

"Is this post-mortem blood pooling, or something else?" Drew pointed to the wrist, almost touching it.

"Hmm, not likely to be post-mortem but can't say really, bit odd, quite a nasty mark there, something just short of a burn looks to me." Dr. Austin had circled her hand around the wrist and was holding the dead woman's arm up between them. "Might know more when the blood work's done." Dr. Austin dropped the wrist a little too quickly, and the victim's arm dropped with an alarming thud onto the steel table. The sudden sound made Drew turn her head, and she found herself staring nose to nose with the doctor.

"Okay, then, I think I've seen enough." Drew slid out first followed closely by Dr. Austin.

"So, Doctor, when will the blood work be done, and when are you planning to recover the bullets?"

"Recover the bullets? Hadn't thought a bit about that, I must say. Recover the bullets? What on earth for?"

"Because we're conducting an investigation, is that not a routine part of an autopsy?" Drew looked at Stephen.

"I suppose. I've no idea really. Is it? Seems a bit odd to me. I thought the constable shot her. Some mystery about that, then?" Dr. Austin looked at her watch for the fourth time.

"Yes, that's our understanding. But to fully understand the sequence of events, we need you to recover the bullets."

"Then, we shall, " Dr. Austin tossed her lab coat over a chair.

"Okay, when can we speak again? I have a few more questions, and we really need the lab results as soon as possible. We'd like to get the medicals wrapped up today."

"You Americans, always in a hurry." Dr. Austin fished around in her pocket for a moment, then handed Drew a small orange card that read *Tangle, Clothing Optional Boating for Women Only, Come Cruise With Us*. "Meet me here. I'll be bringing her in about ten-thirty after the last cruise. I'm off, then."

Chapter Five

The light drizzle had turned into a more serious rain, and Drew and Stephen ran under the shop overhangs, a strategy that kept them dry until the overhangs ended halfway down Commercial Street. They ducked into a corridor of shops in search of an umbrella.

"A doctor who gives boat rides to naked girls; you don't see that every day." Stephen shook the rain off his spiral pad. "Geez, my notes are a mess now."

"I know. Was she stunning or what? I thought I was going to pass out in there. And not from the smell of formaldehyde." Drew began to wipe her sleeve on a store window in an effort to see if they might have umbrellas. "Forget it. This is just expensive plastic crap. How many clever salt and pepper shakers do people need anyway?"

"Oh, my god. You noticed. I can't believe it. Oh, good, coffee. Can we?" Stephen stepped through the door of Grind This, a clear competitor of Grind, which, they found out later, was opened by the owner's ex-boyfriend.

"Noticed what? I'm in for a latté, decaf, don't forget."

"Yeah, like I'd make that mistake." Stephen ordered the coffee. "The doctor. Noticed the doctor. I can't believe you actually noticed a woman. There may be hope for you yet."

"What's not to notice? She's like drop dead gorgeous. No pun intended. First interesting woman I've met in a long time. Plus the whole accent thing just makes me weak in the knees. Okay, we can spare twenty minutes to play. Then I want to go see the photos, and we need to run down the vet. I want to know more about that dog. Let's go in here." Drew stepped through the door of Looking Glass gallery dealing mostly in fine art photography. "What's with the accent anyway? British? Australian? What do we think?" Drew drifted toward the back room of the gallery. Framed pieces were stacked in neat rows along the bottom of the walls. "What is this, like the bargain bin part of the gallery? Never seen that before." Drew began mindlessly flipping through the stacked pieces. "Some of this stuff is really nice."

"Oh, yeah. This is nice." Stephen held up a large black and white photograph of two naked men shot from behind, arms linked, walking into Barney's department store in downtown Manhattan.

"Gives a whole new meaning to retail, dear." Drew moved to a new stack. "You know, I just don't see this job as being done by our girls from New York. Nothing about this really clicks for me. Sure is bizarre in its own right, though, I must say. I think we'll know for sure once we see those pictures. Oh, my god, Stephen, look what I found. Look at this!" Drew held out a black steel frame surrounding what was clearly recognizable as artist Keith Haring's "Radiant Baby" icon in bright red.

"Holy shit! What's that doing in here? Let me see. Is it an original? Can't be, it's only like two thousand dollars. It must be a litho. Still that's a good price. Go find out, I'm going to see if I can find another one."

Drew took the piece to the front of the store. "Excuse me, but do you know what this is?"

"Sure do, honey, it's a picture," the woman said, laughing the suburban-bridge-club laugh of a late middle-aged woman who had spent a life as a clerk in shopping mall retail.

"Uh, right. But can you tell me if it's an original or a lithograph? Do you know this is a Keith Haring?"

"Sure, hon, says right here on the label on the back, Keith Haring, lithograph. Baby, it's kinda cute. Ya like it? If ya got it in back there, it's half price. Shipping's extra, though."

"But this is a Keith Haring, why isn't it up front with the rest of the finer art?" Drew set the Haring gently on the counter and began fishing for her wallet.

"He's not a local artist. Only local artists go up front. Here, fill this out for the shipping; it's an extra twenty-five for that. Be there in about a week or so. That good enough for ya? Gonna be back home by then, are ya?"

"Uh, yes, that's fine. A week would be great." Drew signed the credit card receipt quickly, certain that at any moment, the gallery owner would return and discover what Drew was sure was a mistake in pricing.

"Okay, all set then. Enjoy it." The woman pointed toward the back end of the gallery. "Looks like you bought that just in time; your husband is looking for ya."

Drew turned. Stephen was standing in the archway holding a framed black and white photograph. The photograph was of two female lovers. The first was lying face up on a bed of white linen. She was visible from the shoulders to mid-thigh. Her Levi's were open and slung low on her hips. Her back was arched, arms extended to her sides, palms down. Her lover was nude, shown from the waist down, walking up her body. One perfectly muscled leg stood straight, foot placed delicately on her lover's hip bone. The other leg was arched, foot pointed down, toes just hidden under the hem of her lover's T-shirt that she lifted lightly to reveal one small perfect breast. The word "Trust" was written in script along the bottom.

"Whoa, it's brilliant. It has such a quiet but powerful eroticism. Maggie would love that. Nice find. But what are you doing with naked girl pictures? You thinking of crossing over again? Hey, I bought the Haring and how jealous are you?" Drew shoved her wallet back into her briefcase. "Come on if you're buying it. Play time is over, I'm afraid. On the upside, I think it stopped raining."

"Drew, come here, you need to see the back. It's hers." Stephen turned the photograph around and pointed to the gold gallery label on the back. "I mean it, come look at this."

Drew started forward and looked at the label. She took the photograph out of his hands and turned it back around. Squinting, she saw the tiniest signature in the bottom right corner, "Maggie Malone." She said nothing. Stephen looked at her with a blend of alarm and sympathetic hope. She stood. Silent. Staring. Blinking. Staring. "Stephen, this is Maggie's work. Maggie took this picture. What does that mean? She's here? On Cape Cod?" Drew rushed the photograph forward to the saleswoman. "Do you know this one? Maggie Malone, the photographer. Do you know where this came from?"

The woman squinted slightly over her reading glasses. After the sale of the Haring, she had returned her attention to her *People* magazine. "Hmm, don't know her right off hand. But I think we got lots more of her stuff upstairs. Looks a lot like it anyway. I could be wrong. All these pictures start to look alike if ya know what I mean. You're more'n welcome to take a look. You gonna take this one, too?"

The woman had been wrong. The pictures upstairs were by Judy Francesconi and, while exquisitely beautiful, did not look even remotely like Maggie's work. Drew and Stephen had scoured the gallery but could find only the one photograph, which Drew now held under her arm.

"So she's here you think? In Provincetown? Or you think she's just selling here? I can't believe she's selling her pictures. She never did that before." Drew nodded to the M&Ms, who were naked and busying themselves draining and cleaning the hot tub under the back stairs.

"She never needed her own money before. Why wouldn't she come here anyway? She loves this place. How could you not have thought that this is exactly where Maggie would come?"

"I don't know, I guess I just thought she'd go somewhere else, someplace farther away from me like San Francisco." Drew unwrapped the package and set the photograph on the kitchen table, angling it against the wall.

"San Francisco? I hate to break it to you, Drew, but Maggie is way too old for San Francisco. That's a town for baby dykes. Besides, it's way too expensive for a starving artist. You have to be really well connected to get a show there."

"Why the hell didn't she just tell me that so I could stop worrying? I think after ten years, I deserve that much. Do you think she's really here? Like right now?" Drew set up up her laptop and reached for the envelope that had been delivered by the evidence technicians.

"Probably because she thought you'd come and find her. She needs space. It's not like she hasn't been telling you that. It's not like there weren't signs."

"Signs? There were no signs. What are you talking about? Everything was fine as far as I knew, then, boom, she's gone." Drew inserted the disk into the computer and began searching the pictures of the bank. "Stephen, come look at this."

"Of course there were signs. Like highway billboards. I saw them, and I wasn't even looking for directions. You just didn't see them because you were never home. And even when you were home, you weren't really home. Face it, you suck at relationships." Stephen moved to sit beside Drew and peered into the computer screen. All he could see were a series of pictures of segments of white stone. "What's this again? What am I supposed to be looking for?"

Drew pushed him so hard he almost fell off the chair. "I suck at relationships? Nice. Actually, I've only had just the one. At least I have the one. Had one. Whatever. I knew this would all come around to being my fault. What wasn't my fault anyway? You think I'm a workaholic, but ya know, somebody in the family had to actually generate an income. This is the floor from the bank. Remember, I asked Whinman to shoot it from where the victim was to the rail where the gun was found." One by one, Drew began to enlarge the pictures so each one filled the screen for several moments.

Stephen pushed off the counter and righted his chair. "Hey, no pushing. Nobody said it was your fault. You women and your obsession with finding fault. It's one of your gender's most unattractive qualities. See that's the problem right there, and you still don't get it. Maggie's not like you. She's fragile. She needs constant care and attention, constant reassurance, constant ego stroking. You on the other hand...well, let's just say you're

43

different from that. You cast a wide shadow. You take up all the space in your life. There was no room for Maggie. I don't see anything in these pictures except for a few blood spatters. These are no help at all."

"I always find it an interesting criticism that I work too hard. When did having goals become a negative character trait anyway? What was I supposed to do, put my career on pause to sit home and make sure Maggie was getting enough ego stroking to get through the day? If I wanted to do that, I'd have married a man. That's exactly right, look, this floor is clean, not a mark on it. We got 'em."

"Got 'em? How do we got 'em?"

"If a .22-caliber hand gun slid five feet across a white slate floor, don't you think there would be scratches in the floor? Slate is pretty easy to scratch, especially if it's white. But here, not one mark. They're lying. No gun slid across this floor. I think he planted it. Now why does a small-town cop in a resort town carry a throw-away piece? Those witnesses were lying sacks of shit." Drew closed the cover to the laptop and stared absentmindedly at the photograph on the table. "Who do we think is the weakest link in that chain?"

"You go see the doctor. I'll go squeeze Mango."

Chapter Six

The interior of Lucky was dimly lit. It was a small bar by Provincetown standards, especially for a performance space. It was full, even at this early evening hour. Men of all ages in leather and Levi's stood angled against the crowded bar rail drinking bottles of beer and glancing alternately at the gay porn on the video monitors and one another.

Stephen first approached the bartender, who said Mango would likely not arrive until fifteen minutes before his show was set to begin at eleven-thirty. Stephen paid for a club soda and wove his way through the crowd to the corner of the bar to wait.

Tangle was easy for Drew to spot even in the pink and blue evening light on McMillan Wharf. It was a forty-five-foot cabin cruiser, whose rails were strewn with twinkling pink and blue party lights. The passengers were still departing, clutching their binoculars and cameras. Dr. Austin was busy securing the boat for the night. She looked up and smiled as Drew approached.

"Solve the big mystery yet?"

"No, afraid not. We still need to talk. Nice boat."

"Come on, then, on you go. Just take a tic to finish tying her up."

Drew felt more than a little out of place sitting in the lounge chair on the deck of the boat, still dressed in her suit. "So have you been doing this a long time? Cruising? I mean on the boat."

"Yes to both, actually. Been here about three years now. Just a bit of luck really, had a friend from medical school who owned her. She had to go back to Mother England rather on the short. So I took over the boat and her little tourist practice."

"So you are from England. We weren't sure."

"Yes, I am. Went to university there, then came to your Harvard. Fell in love with this place then. Used to come up on weekends. Ferry took a lot longer then than it does now. I think this is the only place in America where people act sensibly. You from Washington, then? I'm on for a bit of wine. Have some?"

"Sure. Just a little, though, I still have quite a bit of work to do. Yes, from Washington now, really from Chicago. Been in D.C. only a few years."

"Ah, here we are then." Dr. Austin set the wine glasses on the small white table between their chairs. "And your lover, does she live there with you? Or am I wrong about that, too?"

"Actually, I came here to talk about the autopsy, Doctor. But just for the record, no you weren't wrong. I do have a lover. Although I can't see why that matters." Drew sipped a tiny bit of wine, placed the glass back on the table, and began fishing in her pocket for her notebook.

"Matters to me. I never go to the trouble of making dinner for anyone I have no chance of bedding. You Americans are a funny lot. You all have these big parades once a year, run round half naked, and the rest of the year, you go about hanging in the closet. Odd lot, indeed. You like pasta, don't you? All of you seem to. I'll put the boil on, then."

"Actually, it's 'in the closet,' we don't actually hang in there. And you have no chance of bedding me, I'm quite taken. I don't really have time for dinner anyway. Did you finish the autopsy? How many bullets did you find? Did you get the blood toxicology?"

"So in a hurry. So many questions. No chance at all? There's always some chance, however small. You fancy me, that's clear already. You American girls always make such a big deal out of casual shagging. Don't understand it really. So serious about something so simple. In England, we're always ready for a go.

Besides, I never discuss work before dinner, so you've no choice really. Just another sec anyway. I like it al dente. Be a love, will you, and turn this off in exactly three more minutes. Just off to take a quick shower, then back in a tic." Dr. Austin disappeared behind a weathered red maple door.

Drew pulled out her cell phone, dialed Stephen's number, and walked over to stand by the Easy Bake Oven-sized stove. "Hey, it's me. Did you find him?"

"No, I'm still waiting at the bar. His show starts at eleven-thirty. So it looks like I'll be here a while. And how is the gorgeous doctor doing? Did she finish with the body? Have you started on her body yet?" Stephen laughed a little too hard at his own joke and coughed club soda up his nose.

"Yeah, right. Actually, she's in the shower, and I'm stirring her pasta. We haven't really talked yet, either. Apparently, we have to follow the British rules and only talk over dinner. We were right, by the way—London. She thinks I 'fancy' her. There is serious tension in the air. Good thing I'm married. Did you check messages? Anybody call yet about the prints on the suspect? Did the vet call back? We're scheduled to interview Billy Boy at ten tomorrow morning. I'd really like to have the rest of it wrapped up by then. What is all that groaning noise in the background? What kind of bar are you in anyway?" Drew turned off the burner and gave the pasta a final few stirs.

"Oh, sorry, I'm standing under the video monitor. Gay porn. Fancy her, eh? I fancy her and I'm gay. And technically you aren't married, you're separated. No, no messages. We probably won't hear about the vet or the prints till tomorrow. I'll check again later, though, just in case. She's in the shower? Well, you clearly got the better end of this deal. I'll call you when I know something. When are we making a Maggie plan?"

"A Maggie plan? I don't know. Been thinking about nothing else really, but I have to keep it together long enough to wrap this up. But if this goes the way I think it will, we'll be turning this over to the state police as a local matter. Anyway, I can't talk anymore right now, she's coming." Drew hung up.

"I see you've at least taken your jacket off. Real progress,

I'd say. You should really do something about that. Can't solve a mystery when you stick out like a sore finger." Dr. Austin stood in the doorway. Her hair still carried a sheen of water and, at this angle, a small spark of light. Her light gray midriff T-shirt that read "Contents Under Pressure" was damp and clinging in the front enough to reveal two small perfect breasts, nipples responding to the cool breeze off the water. Small rivulets of water drizzled in starts and stops down her tan stomach until they disappeared under the band of her black oversized Joe Boxer women's boxer shorts that were so large that, as she walked forward, it appeared they might fall off.

"Wow, I needed that. Cold shower, too, lucky for you. Hard piloting all those naked women around, gets me a bit charged up, truth be told. Ah, the pasta's perfect. Okay then, off with you. I'll serve. Do bring the wine, though, I've only just the two hands."

Drew picked up the bottle and stumbled to the table feeling somewhat woozy from the water and the view. She unbuttoned the first two buttons of her blouse and began rolling up her sleeves. As Dr. Austin leaned in closer than necessary to set the plate of pasta in front of her and filled her wine glass, she clung desperately to her sleek black Mont Blanc pen to steady herself.

"Okay then, here's the skinny on our girl there. Recovered four bullets. Since I don't play with guns myself, I don't know what kind. I brought them in a sack. They're in there." Dr. Austin pointed to the red maple door. "You can figure that out, I suppose. They all came out of the chest except one that was imbedded in the upper sinus. That's it, really, except for all the work she had done. You Americans and your vanity. Quite a project she was. Oh, and the tox screen was negative." Dr. Austin stopped talking long enough to slowly sip a long piece of linguine into her mouth.

"How did it get into the sinus cavity? There were no entrance wounds there. Did it ricochet? What do you mean a lot of work? You mean like plastic surgery?" The table was so small that as Dr. Austin slurped the last of her linguine, she flung small spots of red sauce onto the front of Drew's shirt.

"Oh, dear. Sorry about that. I've grown feral living on this boat. Not fit for human company really. Best take that right off before it sets."

Drew looked down at her shirt, now wishing she had packed more carefully for this trip. "Well, uh, I can't really do that. Do you have any club soda? I think that works."

"Don't be silly, I'll just run and get you a T-shirt. I have fifty or so. We'll soak it. Be out in a tic."

Dr. Austin brought back a huge oversized blue T-shirt with *Tangle* emblazoned across the front in black. "There, then, all set. Let me have that one. I'll have it soak while we move on to dessert." Dr. Austin stood holding the T-shirt in her hand. A long silence fell between them. Not the conspiratorial kind or the large thudding kind that drops down between distant relatives at a family reunion. This was the kind of silence that alternately crackled and sparked like a soft mist landing on embers.

Dr. Austin reached over and unbuttoned the third, then fourth button on Drew's shirt. Drew protested at first and pushed her hands away. But when Dr. Austin tried a little more forcefully, Drew sat still in the chair and let her. She let her unbutton all the buttons one by one, slide her fingers just below the waistband, and lift the shirt slowly out of her pants to get to the last one. Drew leaned forward to allow her to slip the shirt off. As she did, she grazed each breast in turn and each responded. Drew continued looking down at her now empty plate.

"Hmm, a bit of sauce bled through, I see. We best take this off, too, shall we?" Dr. Austin whispered into Drew's ear as she unhooked her bra from the front and let it slide down Drew's arms. Drew grabbed it a little harder than she intended and pulled it partway back up.

"Dr. Austin, I don't think you really understand how much this isn't going to happen."

"At this point in the evening, I think it's only right you call me J.J.," Dr. Austin whispered as she succeeded in slipping the bra from Drew's hands. She paused as she knelt between Drew's legs. Then she rose and moved around behind her, and began to slip the T-shirt over Drew's head. As she grazed Drew's breasts, a soft moan escaped before Drew could stifle it. She felt a soft trail of kisses cascading down her neck. The T-shirt was so oversized,

J.J. was able to slip most of her head underneath it from the side, continuing the now firmer kisses all the way to Drew's breastbone. She felt her weakness rising.

"Oh, god, I so cannot. I so cannot. You need to come out of there." Drew reached her arm up in an attempt to pull J.J.'s head back out of the shirt, but when she felt J.J. making firm contact with her right nipple, instead she pulled J.J.'s head closer. J.J. reached down and unbuttoned, then unzipped Drew's pants. She attempted to slide one finger beneath the waistband of her underwear. Drew caught her firmly by the wrist.

"Schlept in fin," J.J. said, mouth still full of hardening nipple.

"Schlept in fin?" Drew started to chuckle and broke back through the surface, and she was hit with the reality that she was more than half naked lying on a boat about to be finger-fucked by a key witness. She sat bolt upright.

"Let me in." J.J.'s words hung in the air.

"No, no, no, no. I can't. We can't. God, I'm sorry, J.J. But I can't. I don't know what's wrong with me. Must be the wine and, well, you. Look at you. You're like the perfect, you know, every part just. Wow. I mean Jesus." Drew put her head heavily in her hands and sat forward in the chair. "I should have stopped you at the very beginning. But as I said, I'm very taken. Damn, why is that again? But anyway, even if I wasn't, which I am, you're a witness. Now you were going to tell me about some plastic surgery, is that right?" Drew wiped the sweat from the side of her face with the end of the T-shirt.

J.J., who had not moved from her position behind Drew, leaned down again and began to whisper in her ear. "Umm-hmm she had heaps of it." Drew felt the soft kisses return.

"Nose, cheek bones, jaw, eyes." Random kisses, small bites, long strokes of smooth tongue. "Breast reduction, don't see that much in America. She was new from top to bottom. Lot of bother to end up so ordinary looking, I'd say." Kisses, harder, the insistence of teeth, tongue. *Don't forget to breathe.*

"Had she been in an accident?" *Words, I need words. Come on, I know a lot of words.* "She didn't seem wealthy. Doesn't that much plastic surgery cost a fortune?" *If you don't stop soon, I'm going to come just from that.* "So an accident?" The involuntary arch of her back. J.J. took Drew's hand and brought it down to where her own hand had been just moments before. Drew pulled her hand away.

"No, no accident. They were recent breaks, one time only." J.J. wrestled Drew's hand back to place. "Apparently, there was nothing she liked about herself, poor thing." Kisses descending, hands, tongue, teeth, hands. Drew felt her resistance swirling and thinning like smoke in a jar. Lost now to everything but the release rising within her. "She cost more than a new house." Drew reached her arm around and pulled J.J.'s mouth hard to her own. As she felt her muscles contract, she held J.J. to her, kissed her hard, harder. As the final forceful moaning groan left Drew's mouth, J.J. swallowed it whole.

They stayed that way for a long time, then began to slowly disentangle.

"There we are then, love. Much better." J.J. kissed Drew gently on top of the head, then began to collect the dishes. "If you care to straighten up as they say, the bathroom's right through that door."

It took Drew a few steps to regain her balance, but she finally made her way to the bathroom. She rearranged her clothing several times, trying to decide if that feeling still lingering in the pit of her stomach, like lottery ping pong balls swirling furiously in the cylinder just before the draw, was giddiness or deep regret.

She wiped the beginnings of tears from her eyes, attempted to avoid making eye contact with herself in the mirror, and washed her hands. She stopped outside the bathroom and leaned heavily against the wall. She stared straight ahead, blinking repeatedly in an attempt to forestall more crying. Then she opened her eyes for the final time and began to squint in the dim light of the hallway.

"What's that?" She bent forward to get a better look in the bedroom across from her without entering. It was hung right over the mattress with a small light underneath illuminating it. She bent a little farther into the room to make sure. "No."

It was the same picture Drew had just purchased at the gallery.

51

In the border, on the bottom was written, "J.J., You're Beautiful, All my love, Maggie."

Chapter Seven

"You fucked a witness? Are you out of your mind? You just jeopardized this whole investigation. My god, what were you thinking? You better hope she never tells that story. If I'd done that, you'd have hung my balls from town hall. I can't believe you did that. Hey, this is kind of fun, I never get to yell at you. And another thing, was she fabulous? I'm so proud of you. Did she make you call her captain? Out with it, sister, I want full details." Stephen was tying his shoelaces.

"I did not fuck a witness. Please stop saying that." Drew continued to pace the floor. "And you're missing the whole point of the story."

"Oh, please. Nice try at parsing that shit. That was totally fucking. Well, girl-fucking anyway. Are you telling me there's something that's the point of the story besides that?" Stephen flipped his necktie under his collar and began the elaborate steps of tying a Windsor knot.

"It is not. Stop saying that. We were not 'girl-fucking' as you say. Listen to me. Yes, there's something more important. Did you not hear the part about the picture? I'm completely freaked." Drew sat at the kitchen table and began guzzling coffee.

"Picture? No. What picture? I must have had the hair dryer on. And listen, everybody needs sex, and you've been without for a long time. You don't have to pretend or justify. I know you too well. You can't own up to the fucking part because you think it's cheating. Well, it's not cheating on your spouse if they leave you first." Stephen grabbed the coffee cup from Drew's hand and set it on the counter. "And enough of this. First of all, it's not decaf and, two, no amount of coffee can erase that orgasm, honey. Just deal with it before your head explodes. Okay, now what picture?"

Drew told him the whole story. "So what does it mean, that she has the original of this picture with 'You're Beautiful' written on it? Is she sleeping with her? Is she her new girlfriend? What are the odds of this? Stephen, help me, I'm completely freaked here."

"Oh, my god. You think you fucked the woman that's sleeping with Maggie? Finally, lesbians doing something interesting enough to talk about at brunch. My brethren will be so jealous." Stephen placed his hand over his heart.

"Again, and for the final time, I did not fuck her. And you're supposed to be helping me, not judging me. Remind me not to call you if my house is ever on fire."

"Who's judging? What exactly had you cooked up in your head that I would say about this? First you tell me you slept with Captain Underpants, then you tell me you think Captain Underpants is sleeping with Maggie, then you ask me to analyze it for you. Analyze it? I can hardly even absorb it. I feel faint."

"Oh, for crying out loud, don't go all Rita Hayworth on me. Not now. I need your help."

"Okay, okay. I'm calming down. Pulse returning to normal zone." Stephen placed his finger on the inside of his wrist. "Well, hell, I don't know. I'm not prepared for this. It's not like there's a precedent. These kinds of things just don't happen to you. This is just so not your life. I'm totally at a loss. It's like we've changed places. You go off and have this wild sexual adventure and I sit in a bar all night waiting to reinterview a witness. That sack of shit never showed, by the way. I think the bartender tipped him off. At a minimum, we know that you have to go back there and find out. You do know that?"

"Go back? Go back and do what exactly?"

"Well, not what you did last night, that's for sure. I mean, at least until you know if she's, you know, with Maggie."

"How's that supposed to happen exactly? How do I start that conversation?"

"We'll figure it out. In the meantime, tick-tock, sister, justice calls." Stephen pointed to his watch. "We need to go or we'll be late with our interview with Officer Billy Bob Joe whatever. Come on, Drew, focus."

"Okay, okay. Yes, you're right. Let's go see if we can ruin someone else's day."

Officer William Baychamp showed up to his interview sporting casual clothes and a very experienced and, one might presume, expensive lawyer. Drew and Stephen led him through the series of events at least half a dozen times. He did not waver. In fact, he didn't vary his account by one word in any of the retellings.

According to him, he was working his usual weekend shift at the normally quiet bank. All of a sudden, the door flew open, banging several times against the wall, a woman with the dog nipping at her heels ran in and began screaming at the top of her lungs, "Give me the money, Give me the money." He drew his weapon, and at the same moment, she pointed a black gun at him, he heard her cock it, then he fired his weapon and kept firing until he discharged all his rounds. Once he had secured the witnesses, he called for backup and an ambulance.

"So now let me see if I've got this just one more time, Officer. You picked up this .22 after it flew out of the suspect's hand, hit on the floor, slid across the floor, and came to rest by the side rail. That right?"

Baychamp nodded as Drew laid the eleven photographs of the floor in front of him one by one. "Officer, these are photographs that were taken yesterday of that part of the floor. Do you notice anything unusual about them?"

Baychamp and his lawyer spent several minutes examining the photographs. "Looks just like a bunch of white space to me," Baychamp said.

"Officer, even computer-enhanced versions of these photographs don't show a single scratch on this section of the floor. Now I know that you planted a throwaway. What I don't know is why. Plus there are no prints or blood on the gun. If you're gonna cough it up, Officer, and tell us how this was some kind of mistake, now would be the time for that. After today, we turn it over to state troopers, and it's out of our hands. You wasted a lot of the government's time here, Billy."

Baychamp looked at his lawyer. "Ms. Morgan, Mr. Shaunessey, I would like to speak privately to Officer Baychamp. If you wouldn't mind waiting outside," Baychamp's lawyer said.

Drew and Stephen had been waiting about fifteen minutes when Baychamp's lawyer emerged. "He's writing it up now. Basically, it's the same story he told you except that after he shot her, he figured out what he thought was the gun was really just a black umbrella wrapped around her wrist. I guess as she came in the door, it flipped up and made a clicking sound. He thought in good faith it was a gun. He panicked. He's just a kid. Anyway, looks like it's not got anything to do with the bank jobs you're chasing. This is going to take a while; he's still coming to terms with it. He always wanted to be a cop and now he probably won't be anymore."

"I hope there's more to the story than that, counselor. There are a few more things about this case that don't click. Tell him to help himself out here and not make any more creative mistakes."

Drew and Stephen crossed over Commercial Street and headed down Bradford.

"What an idiot. How did he think he could actually pull that off? That guy is dumb as a box of hair. Did you see him clinging to that St. Christopher medal around his neck? What does he think, St. Christopher is the patron saint of liars?" Stephen fished in his pocket for the address. "We're going the wrong way, it's that direction."

"Yes, he does think that. Because God said, 'Please stay stupid till I get back.' Kind of funny, though, don't you think, that he'd have a high-priced Boston lawyer in here overnight. Funny connections for a rookie beat cop to have. Well, it's not our problem anymore. Let's just wrap up this last detail. I still need a plan to see Austin again. Maybe wrapping the case will give me the opening I need. That should be easy. 'Doctor, the investigation has wrapped, thanks for the great orgasm, and by the way, are you doing my wife?' Yes, that's exactly the right approach."

The vet's wife answered the door of the white clapboard house. Through the screen door, she told Drew and Stephen that her husband was not home because he had been called to tend to a sick horse in New Bedford, more than an hour away.

"Great, that rearranges the whole rest of the afternoon," Drew said.

"This is the only break that we know we're going to get while we're here, so let's go change, then let's go."

"Go? Go where?" Drew said.

"What do you mean where? To see the infamous Captain Underpants, of course. To get the story."

"No fucking way. Way no fucking way. Are you nuts? I'm not going back over there now. Maybe not ever."

"What are you talking about? Of course we're going over there. Are you out of your mind? Of course you have to find out. Not knowing is killing me. I mean killing you."

"Oh, my god. I do. But I can't. I don't think you fully comprehend the full panoply of last night's events. Any conversation now would just define awkward."

"Okay, then I'll go talk to her."

"Yeah, that'll happen."

"Why not?"

"And how would that go exactly? Hello, remember me? I'm Drew's friend and I was just in the neighborhood, even though you live on a boat and therefore, by definition, don't even live in a neighborhood, and thought I would stop by to say hello and casually ask you if you're shagging my friend's ex-girlfriend. God, I can't believe I just said ex-girlfriend."

"Wow, I can't believe you just said ex-girlfriend." Stephen said at the same time. "What's shagging?"

"I think it's British for fucking."

"Ah, the dream of a common language. And no, I would just tell her I want to see her boat, and when we walked past the picture, I would casually ask how she acquired it and it would go from there. I spend a lot of time in bars, I can easily speak drivel to someone I don't know at all, hoping for a positive outcome. I believe it's called dating."

"No. No way. I need some time to think here. This is just too soon. I need some time to take this apart and put it back together before I could ever be prepared to go over there again. As weirdly awful as the questions are, I'm terrified that the answers will make me feel worse. I mean, what if? Okay, I can't think about that right now. I need some air."

"You need some Prozac."

"Yeah, maybe later. Right now I just need time and oxygen."

Chapter Eight

Drew veered over to Commercial Street and headed to the wharf. *Tangle* was docked, J.J. was lying on the deck, her body slick with sweat and salt as she raised and lowered herself in a series of quick sit-ups. As her elbows rose to touch her knees, her teal boxer shorts parted at the legs, revealing what lay beneath.

"I thought you'd probably just be getting in now," Drew said.

J.J. stopped her sit-ups briefly and looked up, smiling slightly.

"We're in for a spot of rain. See that halo round the sun there? Means rain in a few hours. We've taken our last ride today. You here for a cruise, then?" J.J. resumed her sit-ups.

"Look, I know this is awkward, but I need to talk to you about something. Something very important. Do you have a few minutes?"

"More serious than death? Come on, then." She held out her hand to help Drew onboard. Even that brief contact produced the same spark as the night before.

"Actually, the shooting seems to be resolving itself. I'm here about something else."

"To reciprocate?" J.J. stood against the rail, arms akimbo, sweat dripping from her face and arms.

"Uh, well, uh, no. I mean, well, I guess I have some explaining to do. And it was. Well. So. I mean, look right at you…it's you're...so...well, perfect. Well, not perfect. Well, yeah, actually perfect pretty much covers it. You. God, I'm sorry, I sound like I'm channeling Diane Keaton. I mean, last night was...well, I don't know...if that's what losing your mind feels like, then I guess I'm ready. No. Not really. Unless really I am. I feel like I am. Losing my mind, that is. Well, no, actually hoping I'm not or won't have to. God, please stop me. Anyway, I just have something I need to ask you."

J.J. started to laugh. "Yes, please do stop. I think I understand. You're dripping with morning-after regret, are you? Here to beg amends and seek absolution so you can face the girlfriend? All right then, you're hereby absolved," she said, making the sign of the cross in the air. "I must say, though, love, based on last night, that girlfriend of yours is falling down. But there you go, absolved. And here's something I've never said the morning after, your bra and bullets are in the bedroom. Come on, let's fetch them out."

When they got to the bedroom, Drew walked over to the picture. "I know this is incredibly awkward. Believe me, I know. And I'm trying hard to sound a whole lot less stupid than I just did. Can I just ask you...this picture, do you know her? The photographer? Did she sign this at a gallery or something? Or do you know her? Maggie."

"What? That picture? Well, yes, I know her. What an odd question. I don't let just anybody snap me in the nude, love. Lot of going on about a simple photo."

"What do you mean snap you?"

J.J. held up her hands as if snapping an air camera.

"Oh, god, that's you? On the bottom? Oh, my god, that is you."

"Yes, the one and only time. Only Maggie could talk me into being snapped as a bottom. Sort of a kick, though, having her walk up me like that. Very sexy, you should try it sometime. You all right there?"

"That's Maggie? Of course." Drew peered more closely at the picture.

"I'm lost here; care to share all the fuss about the picture?"

"That's Maggie."

"Right. And?"

"That's my Maggie. That's my girlfriend." Drew slumped onto the bed.

"Are you having me on? I don't think so, love. She can't be your girlfriend, she lives here. Has for months."

"It's her. We're, well…separated, sort of. For months? How many months? How well do you know her? Never mind, I guess the picture tells the whole story."

"That's your girlfriend? Did you know that when you came here last night? That's gruesomely passive aggressive even by American standards. Is this whole thing a ruse then?"

"What? No. What are you talking about? J.J., you examined a dead body, remember? Plus which, there were bullets." Drew held up the bag that held said items.

"Oh, right. Sorry, this whole thing has me somewhat off balance. Yes, all right, we're caught in a karmic revenge cycle or something, aren't we, love. Might take a bit to sort through all this."

"Could you answer one question for me first?"

"So you're the neglectful barrister she keeps going on about. Well, fancy that. No worries, love, I'm not shagging her, if that's what you mean."

"You're not?"

"Shagging Maggie? I'd say not. Don't get me wrong, she's a lovely woman, quite nice and solidly good looking. But she's certainly not my type. She's all soft and flowing. I like my women with a bit more angles and corners and a much more ruthless intelligence. No offense, she's a lovely woman as a friend. Different strokes as they say. Well, we've a bit of a mess here, haven't we? Come on, then. This is a two-bottle conversation. Ever seen the cove up close?"

Drew sat silently in the deck chair. J.J. cast off the lines and eased the boat out of the slip and headed slowly out of the harbor, bow barely wrinkling the water. She wove passed the line of commercial whale watching boats choked with tourists.

"I hate those boats. Funny lot these tourists, all recycling and ecology at home. But once they get here, they're willing to pay any price to see these poor bastards perform. Are you with me there?" Drew was still unresponsive. They floated along in silence until J.J. cut the engine and dropped anchor just at the tip of Herring Cove.

"All right, you just going to sit there like a wounded bird or are we getting on about it?" J.J. took a seat across from Drew and unwrapped an orange Popsicle. "Want half?" She pointed the Popsicle toward Drew.

"No. I mean, no thank you. Getting on about what? Why did you bring me here anyway? Really, J.J., I'd rather be alone."

"Can't do it, love. It's the rescue instinct. Strong in us seafaring types. We're honor bound to help wounded creatures. Besides, you're fairly oozing questions about your Maggie. So out with it. Now that you know we aren't sleeping together, what else do you want to know?"

"How long have you known her? How do you know her? Does she live here now? That's stupid, I guess she does."

"Don't know really how long she's been here. I met her at a gallery opening a bit of a while back. They were showing her pictures. I liked them, of course, all raw sexual power and energy. I thought it was a bit of a contrast, really, her being so low key and all. Interesting woman, though, and quite good looking. So we took on as friends from then." J.J. ran her tongue up and down the outside of the Popsicle, and small drips made their way down her chin and onto her upper chest.

"Where does she live?"

"Up the way a bit, by the Writer's Center. Bit of a haul but a lot of space by our standards. Good for taking pictures is my guess."

"Can you show me?"

"Can, but won't do you much good now. She was off to London last week." J.J. slid the full length of the Popsicle slowly in and out between her lips.

"London? Maggie can't afford London. Besides which, she's scared to death of airplanes. She used to cry all the way over on the Cape Air flight. London. All right, she's in London."

"Well, she must have gotten over that fear. I've a friend there with a small gallery. He's setting her up with a show."

"So she's like a famous artist now? When is she coming back?"

"Don't know, love. Likely she'll be gone at least a couple of months, though."

"Did she go alone? Does she have a girlfriend?"

"Really want to know that, do you?"

"I think so, yes."

"Can't say for sure. A few have tried, I know. But she seems to chase them all away. She can't stop chattering about her last girlfriend."

"Her last girlfriend? You mean me? She refers to me as her last girlfriend?"

"Sort of. It's always a bit blurry when she gets on about it. She sure seems angry, though. How many sins did you commit anyway?"

"A lot apparently. I work a lot. I mean *a lot*. I guess I stopped paying attention. I thought her little excursion was just her way of reeling me back in. I'm such an idiot."

"We all are in that way, I'm afraid."

"So she talks like it's over? For good?"

"Wouldn't want to venture that. Like I said, she's blurry about it."

"Blurry."

"Yes. Can't tell if she's just off on girlfriend holiday or if it's more serious. Don't think she's decided really."

"God."

"What about you, then? Been six months or so, what are you thinking? Just sitting about waiting for her to come to her senses, then?"

"I don't know exactly. I feel like I'm in limbo. I just was waiting for a chance to talk her into coming back home. Ten years is a lot to give up on."

"It's about the time, then, is it? Is that your working lie? You're waiting for your girlfriend pension or something? You think if you make it past a certain point, then there's some kind of guarantee.

I don't think it works that way, love. Even the brightest stars have been known to dim and go cold without warning. Zymborska says it's because they're unencumbered by memory. They don't know everyone's counting on them to always shine on."

"I'm sorry. I have no idea what that means. Who's Zymborska? How pathetic am I? She's out here running around and I'm sitting around every night waiting for the doorknob to turn."

"Well, not last night." J.J. placed her finger on the small remaining amount of Popsicle and drew light circles around her navel. "Sure you don't want some? Great way to cool down."

"I'm trying really hard to be restrained here. Last night. Last night was, well, incredible. I mean you are. I mean, that's apparent, of course. I mean just look at you. My God and all of that. But I can't really do that again, ever. Well, not ever, but, well, you know what I mean," Drew said, eyes on the growing puddle of orange ice on J.J.'s stomach.

"Doesn't sound to me that you even know what you mean. But we'll let human nature be for now. Really think you can control even that, do you? Control everything, then?"

"Well, basically yeah, I guess I do."

"That working out well for you?" J.J. turned the Popsicle stick over on her tongue a final time.

Drew laughed. "Yeah, well, there's that. But anyway, I would like to at least buy you dinner before I leave. As a thank you for all your help. With the case, help with the case. Dinner in a very crowded restaurant."

"Right, then. Just the ticket. Dinner in a crowded restaurant. Can't say I'm not disappointed, though. Revenge fucking being so thorough and all. So is that dinner for two or three?"

"Three?"

"Yes. Me and you or me, you, and Maggie in memory. Shall we just set a place for her, then?"

"Two. Just dinner and just two."

"Very well, we best get in now, I smell the rain coming."

J.J. brought the boat back at full throttle. When they got closer to the breakwater, she motioned Drew forward and slid her between herself and the wheel. She ran her hands through Drew's arms and positioned Drew's hands under hers on the wheel in a tight grip. J.J. leaned in tight, which bent Drew forward at the waist and pressed her against the wheel and the buzz of the engine.

"J.J. I just...um...said. Did you hear anything I just said?"

"Feel the engine? Like trying to tame a wild thing, isn't it? All speed and raw power in your hands. Feel it everywhere, don't you? Feels like you could own this ocean."

The boat lurched suddenly to the left, almost throwing them off-balance. "Careful there. Don't ever be deceived, the water is controlling you. No getting around that. First rule of the sea, nature always wins."

Chapter Nine

Drew was light-headed as she made her way slowly down the pier. Her body still held the scent of J.J. She could still feel the faint echoing press of her thigh and the clinging dampness that remained. She made her way past the few remaining tourists all chattering about whales in full breach. A chill rose in the air as a light mist began to gather itself in earnest. She held herself in a tight hug as a dull nodding sadness attached itself to her.

Droplets of water began to pool and slide down her face, mixing with a steady flow of tears. She edged her way along the inside of the sidewalk, trying to avoid eye contact with the throngs of young couples who passed her on either side. Ribbons of memory unfurled. The early years when she and Maggie would save for months just to be able to buy a new record or a good book for keeping.

The long sessions of urgent early sex, the look on Maggie's face, both prideful and wary, the day Drew graduated from law school. The soft curve of her muscular arms as she struck out during every at-bat the last summer she agreed to play on the softball team. Such a girl. The way she held Maggie the day the news came of her mother's diagnosis. The harshness in Maggie's voice anytime anything approaching harm would come their way. The way Maggie was always on her side in every struggle, every fight, even when she thought Drew was dead wrong. Which was almost never. The way the light attached itself to her when she threw her head back in genuine and giddy laughter. The cacophony of discord about the move to Washington. The high thin silence that followed it. The soft click of a suitcase closing. A final slamming of a final door. The clanging, thrashing angry sound of a broken heart sweeping up after itself. The lies about the truth: She was—is—too self-absorbed, inconsistent, crazy for normal, unsupportive, demanding, weak.

We were too much alike, too different. Breathe. Slow. Shower. Never. Shower a ridiculous number of times. Check my BlackBerry. Buy something, leather jacket? Black. Italian, soft. Something that smells like the inside of a new car. Drive something new. Porsche? No. Beemer? A twenty-year-old? Too clichéd, pedestrian. Drive, though. Top down. Fast. Ask directions to the edge. Travel. Europe. Have a nervous breakdown in seven different languages. Check my BlackBerry. Therapy? Fuck that. Tell me you're fucking life story first, Doctor "I Wasn't Smart Enough To Go To Medical School." Pass my fucking test, then we'll see who figures who out first. Make a note, get emotionally reorganized. Check my BlackBerry.

Drew stood finally in front of the small clapboard house that matched the address J.J. had reluctantly given her. It was a small two-story salt box house. Gone gray now with age, it looked neglected, one shutter gone completely, one hanging at a precarious angle as if it were deciding whether it would stay or go. In the upper window, no doubt captured attic space, sat a neon blue sign that burned the word "artist." Drew sat heavily on the front porch and leaned her head against the rail. Her body began to slowly release itself into the stuttering sobs of full grief. It was the actuality of it. This house had held Maggie behind its wood and nails and chipping splintered porch, beyond the grass, grown long now, just beginning to show signs of its occupant's absence. She ran her hands lightly up and down the length of the porch rail as if she were touching a live thing.

Then, the truth about the truth: I can't believe I managed to hold onto you as long as I did. You. This incredibly beautiful creature who sprinkled light and kindness everywhere, and always smelled like morning. *Were you out of your mind? Picking me?*

This rumbling, tumbling warrior, eyes brimming with revolution. *Really, Maggie, what were you thinking? Besides which, you were way too beautiful for me. And everyone knew it. Think I didn't see all those, "What is she doing with her?" looks.* Smart matters in the outcomes of history, in changing the world's character for the better. In praying for the dead and fighting for the living. It matters, I know. Brains matter in the hard workings of the world. But let's face it, if you want to get the guns off the streets, send Julia Roberts door to door. One kiss, one gun. You'd have them all in ninety days. So that's it then. The comfort of easy explanation. Can I let us off the hook that easily? If only. How did we let ourselves get caught so off-guard? It's not like we didn't know. We did know. That it's not about the eager early promises, the soft curve of muscle, the convincing charm of chemistry. It's about keeping your balance, maneuvering around corners, edges, angles, the invisible borders of a mood; learning that forgiveness isn't submission, that one negative cancer test trumps your twenty worst arguments, that failure isn't final. That it's the dim green light of emergency rooms, getting separated in a crowded and violent protest, light rain falling at a funeral on a cruelly beautiful spring afternoon, a scattering of ashes. We knew. That love without honor can be as short as the life of a dancer. That certain promises are more than an ancient arrangement of language. That when you promise "for better or worse," you can never imagine how bad "worse" can get. That to last, love must be soft and steady as the breathing of birds, strong and sure as the tattered, weathered wings of an angel.

The rain was a robust and steady stream now. Drew, soaked through, stumbled to her feet, suddenly made awkward by the weight of her clothes. A small shiver escalated to shaking as she gathered herself to go. Blinking furiously, her eyes caught a flickering glimpse of the only remaining early evening star. She followed its path until the billows of fog swallowed it whole.

Chapter Ten

The vet looked like the vacation postcard version. He was in his mid-sixties, thick through the middle with giant arms and ruddy complexion earned by a life of lazy afternoon fishing. He stood on the porch to his office smoking a pipe and reached out a giant thick hand to Drew.

"Thanks for coming back. Sorry about earlier, it's been a busy day. I have your bullets here, found two. There may be more, but I couldn't bring myself to cut that poor creature up any more than necessary. I will, though, if it's important. Just thought I'd ask first."

"Actually, this seems to be resolving itself. You made the right call. We weren't expecting you to find more than two anyway. I can't tell you how much I appreciate you taking the time to do this for us. I guess we'll be off now." Drew grabbed the plastic bag holding the bullet fragments and turned to leave.

"Wait now, you'll be wanting this, too, I expect." The vet held out a small quarter-inch piece of dull silver metal.

"What is it?" Drew held the piece close to her face trying to read its raised etching.

"It's a police dog. Well, was at some point. Judging by her age, I'd say it's been quite a few years since she saw active duty."

"What? A police dog? Are you sure? What does this have to do with it again?" Drew held up the piece of metal.

"That's the P.D. number. All police dogs get them. They

implant it just under the skin at the scruff of the neck. Don't hurt 'em none, though. It tells you what force they belong to and when they started. Just to keep track of 'em if they ever get loose of ya. Looks like this one was trained in Boston. Guess somebody here adopted her. Sorta surprised the owner hasn't come forward, these are hard dogs to get a hold of. Probably afraid of gettin' sued given what's happened. Anyway, can I dispose of her now? There's not much left."

"Actually, I'm sorry, no, could you hold onto her just until you hear from me? Probably tomorrow. Could you do that for us?"

"Sure thing. Just let me know." The vet disappeared behind the thudding white screen door.

"Okay, what the hell does this mean?" Drew placed the piece of metal in Stephen's palm.

"Well, one thing, it means is that cop is a lying sack of shit. Another thing it means is we need to get to Boston. And right fucking now."

"I don't know about Boston. This is a weird twist for sure, but I still don't see anything federal. In terms of jurisdiction, we are still on pretty thin ice here."

"Right on, well, let's do this. Let's call Spree back at the office and see if she can run down the dog's tag on Interlink. In the meantime, let's find a way to get to Boston. If we go for no reason, we've only lost a couple of hours. If there's a drug connection, then we beat the Boston prosecutors to the punch."

"That makes sense. And of course, I'd love to figure this out before the Boston office gets their claws into it. I'm in, let's get to Boston. Oh, shit, Boston. How the hell are we going to get up there?" Drew looked at her watch. "The high-speed ferry is long gone and we'll never get a Cape Air flight now, and the two rental cars at the airport are taken for the week, I checked when we arrived."Hmm…that only leaves by land. Now who do we know that might be interested in driving us to Boston?" Stephen stood smiling.

"No way. I am not asking her. Besides, she only owns a motorcycle and that's a non-starter."

"She might know someone with a car. Come on, get your courage up, we're losing time here." Stephen handed her his cell phone.

Chapter Eleven

Drew and Stephen waited outside Angel's. They sat on the white stone ledge, and Drew kicked small bits of gravel with the impatience of a child.

"This part where you don't tell me is my least favorite part." Stephen lightly kicked some gravel back in Drew's direction. "Did she dump you overboard or something? I noticed your hair was still wet when we got to the vet's."

"This is me saying nothing."

"It's a long ride to Boston. Am I supposed to be nice to this woman or not? Do we like her or do we hate her? You could tell me that much without telling me if she's rolling around with Maggie. Drew, look at me. Was this a huge mistake? If so, we can find another way up there." Stephen placed his arm gently around Drew's shoulders.

"She's not rolling around with Maggie. They're just friends. Or were. Maggie doesn't even live here anymore. She's like some famous artist now. Flying off to London, or some bullshit, to meet some guy and have some kind of big show or something. How does somebody become a famous artist in six months anyway? I guess her time away from me was well spent."

"Jesus. How do you know all this?"

"From J.J. It's her friend who's doing the show. I saw her house, Stephen. She had a house here. An apartment really, part of a house. Anyway, ya know, she had like a place here. A whole place. A whole other life. People who knew her. Just her. Like people who knew just her and not her and me. Not us. That seems so strange to me. How is that possible? How could she just go and be like this whole other person without me? Just this wild artist girl who runs around barefoot taking pictures and going to parties and meeting people. How could she become just Maggie again so easily?"

"Oh, man. Well, you don't know that it was that easy. It couldn't have been. Maggie was totally in love with you. Maybe she just wanted to show you she had something in her life that was as important to her as your work is to you. You never did take her art all that seriously. Maybe the only way she could find herself was by making this grand gesture. You cast a wide shadow, ya know. Maybe she just wanted to come back to you on her own terms with her own shadow in tow. As Maggie the ... something, the artist maybe. Not just the 'always in progress' Maggie, but as sort of a more finished product."

"Jesus, you make her sound like a science project. But you might be right. Or it might just be that we're done and I'm the only one who doesn't know it. Seems to me that she just rode off into the sunset and never even bothered to look back."

"I think she's looking back right now and wondering the same as you are." Stephen squinted his eyes to avoid the high beam headlights as the car turned up the driveway.

"Good God almighty, what the hell is that thing?" Drew said, shielding her eyes.

Their eyes finally focused on a huge silver Hummer that had attached to its roof a five-foot-by-four-foot metal chicken outlined in bright yellow neon.

"Oh, my god. Did we go to war with Jim Purdue and no one told me?" Stephen said.

J.J. leapt from the driver's seat smiling. "Sorry, best I could do on the short. It's a solid ride, though. Belongs to a friend of mine. Need to have it back to her no later than noon tomorrow. She needs it for a barbeque."

"I am not riding in that. This is serious business we're doing here. I am not, repeat, not riding to Boston in a chicken tank.

What were you thinking?"

"I was thinking you asked me to do you a favor on the spur. Held up my end. Belongs to a friend of mine who owns the Chicken Shack. Free advertising. Hard to sell chicken in a lobster pot town." J.J. bent down to pick up Drew's briefcase.

"That should be on a stamp or something." Stephen opened the door and got in the front passenger seat.

"The chicken is really good, actually. So warm and tender, the warm juice dribbles right down your chin." J.J. paused briefly about an inch from Drew's face, smiled, then walked around to the driver's door. She tossed the briefcase in the back.

"Can't we take it off just for tonight and reattach it tomorrow before we take it back?"

"No, sorry, she's welded solid." J.J. banged her hand hard on the roof, then started the engine.

The rippling muscles of J.J.'s thigh and calf as she shifted gears were enough stimulation to keep Drew awake for the first half hour of the ride. That and the need to prevent any unsupervised conversation between Stephen and J.J. But eventually, the clouds muscled the sun aside and the weight of the day dissolved into sleep.

"So, you letting me in on it, then? Or is it all top secret and whatnot?" J.J. turned the radio down to a barely audible level.

"I guess if Drew didn't tell you, that's because you're still technically a witness, so I guess it's best if you don't have any information that could be seen later as tainting your testimony. The rules are a little tricky and very specific about these kinds of things. Really we shouldn't even have you in the car at all except for the fact that it's your car and all. Usually, we would have just rented a car except that it was too late and it was closed. So under normal circumstances, you wouldn't even be here."

"Goodness. A bloody 'no' would have been sufficient. Looks like a long ride to Boston then for the two of us." J.J. shifted hard into third.

"Oh. Sorry. It's just that I can't afford to make any mistakes right now."

"Can she?" J.J. nodded in the direction of the backseat.

"Can she what?"

"Afford to make any mistakes."

"Is that what you are? A mistake?" Stephen stared at J.J., who stared at the road.

"Ah, now we're on to the point, aren't we?" J.J. turned her head in Stephen's direction and grinned.

"Look, Doc, you seem like a nice enough person, but that one back there is one of the most important stars in my sky."

"Yes, certainly seems so. I'm not out to do any damage. I tend wounds, not cause them. And call me J.J. or Doctor. Calling me Doc makes you sound simple, which you clearly are not."

"Okay, Doctor, fair enough. Well, she does like you, I'll say that much. It's just that she's not always the queen of good decisions. It's her only flaw."

"Her only flaw, eh? Well, I doubt that."

"Well, don't. Not ever." Stephen stared hard at the road ahead.

"Ah, so it is more then. You're in love with her?"

"What? Don't be ridiculous. Love her, of course, with all my heart and always. But 'in love,' not likely. I am, you may have noticed, a homosexual. Doctors—"

"So, just that clean, then? Simple lines. Two sides—girls here, boys there? I think people are more complicated than that. Love and friendship get blurry. Lawyers—"

"Maybe for you. I myself have a totally unblemished record of homo behavior." Stephen punctuated his sentence with an air period.

"If you say so. And what is that beeping?" J.J. opened the console.

"Oh, shit, that's probably Spree." Stephen grabbed the cell phone and mumbled a series of "Uh-huhs" into the mouthpiece while scribbling on the palm of his hand. "Are you sure? Good god. I'll tell her right now. Yes, we're about an hour out now. Yes, got it. And on the other issue? The ID? Nothing? Okay, we'll call you when we get to Boston." Stephen closed the cell phone and slid it into his pocket. "Sorry, Doctor, you were saying...?"

"Was that Spree?" Drew's head appeared between J.J. and

Stephen. "Hi there," Drew said in a soft still sleepy voice to J.J.

"Good morning, princess, and, yes, it was Spree. She made contact. We have identity and location. So if we can make a plan, we're good to go for Operation Boston. We need to talk and that would be right now."

"Stephen, did you become J. Edgar Hoover while I was sleeping? Operation Boston?" Drew leaned in between the seats.

"Somebody needs coffee and no decaf this time." Stephen pointed to a road sign. "J.J., can you pull off just long enough for us to get coffee?"

They pulled into the nearly vacant parking lot and stopped just outside the glass front entrance to The Hole Point. Even at this distance, the air was permeated with the smell of dissolving sugar.

"Oh, my god, what's that smell? It's making my teeth hurt." Drew lightly clasped her hand over her mouth.

"That's The Hole Point." J.J. snapped on the overhead light and began fishing in the front seat for her wallet.

"The whole point of what?" Drew squinted her eyes to make out the interior of the shop. Standing behind the glass counter was a young teenaged boy dressed in a broad orange and white-striped uniform. He wore a hat low on his head that was made up of two oversized doughnuts fixed as eyes, a longjohn placed vertically for a nose and finally seven doughnut holes set in a half circle in a permanent sugary grin. "Oh, I get it. Can anything here be just normal?"

"On the Cape, this is normal." Stephen had jumped from the passenger seat and was bent over in the parking lot stretching his lower back. "J.J., I really need a minute or two to talk to Drew privately. Would you mind going in first?"

"Okay. then. But you don't know what you're missing."

As soon as the three small bells on the shop door pinged signaling that J.J. was out of earshot, Stephen jumped into the backseat of the Hummer. "Brace yourself, sister, I have real news. We got a hit on the dog tag."

"Okay and?"

"Get this. The tag traces to William Baychamp Senior. We

can only presume that he's Billy Butthole's father."

"What the...? Are you kidding me? How?" Drew scribbled notes on the yellow legal pad in her lap. "Are we sure about this?"

"Yes, we are absolutely sure about this. Apparently, he was a Boston P.D. vice detective most of his career. Drug unit. When he retired last year, the dog went with him."

"So wait, what do we think this means? It was the cop's dog that chased her? You think he had the dog in the bank and it just got out of control?" Drew rubbed her temple with the end of her pen.

"But why would the guy shoot his own dog, or more precisely, his dad's dog? How did the dog get there from Boston anyway? Why wouldn't the cop just tell us that?"

"This is still twirly for me. All the witnesses said the dog chased the woman into the bank. They can't all be mistaken. And the only way they would all be lying is if this was some kind of conspiracy." Drew stared at the legal pad and tapped the pen in rhythm in the palm of her hand.

"That group? Conspiracy? That seems out of the question. There definitely are pieces missing, but we need to move on with the pieces we have."

"Okay. You're right, of course. What about an ID on the body? Are we any closer on that?"

"Spree thinks it'll be at least another hour or so. I told her we'd call her from Boston. So now what? Do we move on this guy or what?"

"Yes. We can't wait. If he's involved, he's definitely a flight risk. If he's still in Boston, we need to pick him up now on a material witness warrant. Hand me that, will ya?" Drew reached into her briefcase and began setting up her laptop computer.

"Doesn't that mean we have to involve the prosecutors in Boston?"

"Not necessarily. I have a relationship with a judge up there. If she's around, maybe we can circumvent them." Drew kept her eyes on the computer screen and continued typing.

"And who'll serve the warrant?" Stephen said.

"We will, of course." Drew finished typing and closed the lid to the laptop.

"We will? Serve a warrant? No way. And what are we going to do with the witness exactly? Not to mention he might not actually like the thought of getting arrested and, I don't know, like resist maybe?" Stephen took the laptop from Drew and slid it back into her briefcase.

"Shit. You're right. We have to at least notify the agents for the pickup. Okay, well, I want to at least be there."

"Okay, Xena, whatever you say. Here comes 'Doctor Do Me' bearing caffeine, thank god." Stephen got out of the car and walked over to help Dr. Austin distribute the coffee.

"Here we are, then. Caffeine all around. And I brought a few pastries just in case you changed your mind." J.J. looked back at Drew. Drew noticed a small dab of red jelly snaking its way from the corner of J.J.'s mouth to her lower chin where it hung suspended. "Pastry good" was all she could muster.

They became ensnared in the thick traffic as soon as they hit Boston. They inched their way along the highway for more than an hour before they reached the courthouse. The two agents met them at the door. After the introductions and the jokes about the chicken car had subsided, the agents followed behind them in an unmarked blue sedan. They stopped in front of a large gray-stone near the waterfront.

"Okay, J.J., this is it. Please stay in the car. We should be out in about fifteen minutes. Stephen, let's go."

Drew and Stephen walked up to the front door.

"Now how do you know this woman again?" Stephen said.

"I told you. We went to law school with her. You'll remember her, I'm sure. Hilda Greenwald. Tall redhead. Really smart. She was in our civ pro class." Drew pressed the buzzer.

"Hilda Greenwald? Hmm, okay, if you say so. A tall redhead. I think I'd remember that. You couldn't have been too close if I don't remember her."

"Good enough that she was willing to look at this warrant after hours."

The door opened to reveal a tall reed-thin woman with lipstick red hair cascading well past her shoulders. She was dressed in a tight black rayon jogging suit. "Drew Morgan," was all she said.

"Hilda. Rather, Judge Greenwald, it's great to see you. This is my partner, Stephen Shaunessey. Stephen, this is Judge Greenwald. Thanks for seeing us so late, Judge. We really appreciate it. By the way, this is a beautiful house." Drew and Stephen stepped through the foyer with its high ceiling and exposed brick walls with what surely was very expensive art suspended on wires along every wall.

"Thanks, we love it here. Bought it just last year after my appointment. Nothing like a lifetime job to give you the courage to put down real roots. We needed more room for the kids anyway."

"Kids? Oh, I hadn't heard about that. Congratulations on that, as well as the appointment. No one deserves it more than you do." Drew and Stephen sat in the two large Queen Anne leather chairs across from the large mahogany desk. "How many kids do you have? And who's the lucky...?"

"Man, actually. Surprised?"

"A little." Drew looked briefly at Stephen to gauge his facial expression. Then she reached in her briefcase and withdrew the warrant.

"It was just easier. And, unlike you, I had a choice. He's a really good man. Two kids. Sarah is three and a half and Sammy is two." Hilda took the warrant from Drew and began to read it. "So when did you make the move to Boston? I think I would have heard if you left Washington."

"I didn't, actually. This is related to a case we're working out of D.C. Piece of a possible homicide in P-Town."

"Oh." The judge stared at Drew over her glasses. "So where are the Boston prosecutors? Don't they have an equal interest in this case?"

"We're kind of in a hurry, Judge, and we're afraid if we wait until tomorrow to dot all the i's and cross all the t's, this guy might flee. So we were hoping..." Drew grinned.

"You were hoping that I would agree to sign off on a warrant the prosecutor's office doesn't even know is being served in their district? Why did you think that?" The judge took off her glasses and set them on the desk.

"For old time's sake? Or maybe because that's the guy who refused to hire you at that office, even though you were far more qualified than any of the boys working there." Drew looked at the floor and clasped her hands together in a tight grip.

"You made an interesting calculation there. And as usual, you calculated right." The judge bent her head down and began signing her name. "By the way, how's Maggie? She liking D.C.? Hard to think of that as a town for her." The judge handed the warrant to Drew.

"Actually, we're, well, somewhat separated at the moment. But my understanding is that she's doing greater than ever in my absence." Drew folded the warrant and handed it to Stephen.

"That wouldn't have anything to do with the woman in the chicken car, would it? You'll have to explain that car to me when we have more time."

"I think you know me better than that."

"Actually, I know you exactly that well if memory serves. Well, you have your warrant. But just to be clear, we are even now, right?" The judge led them down the hall back to the front door.

"We were even before this, Hilda, and thank you. I think you may have saved my case." Drew and Hilda shook hands much longer than necessary.

"Okay. What was that about?" Stephen whispered as soon as the door closed behind them.

"Oh, god. It's complicated and another lifetime ago. Let's just say that I knew Hilda in law school in a way that you didn't."

"What? As in know *know*? You cheated on Maggie?" Stephen stopped and looked at Drew.

"Good god, no. How can you even ask me that? I was totally devoted to Maggie. We were just taking a little time off. The stress of the first year of law school was too much for both of us. So we separated for a few weeks." Drew continued walking toward the car.

"You never told me that."

"We didn't tell anyone. We didn't want a lot of free relationship advice. Come on, the agents are waiting."

"So in a few weeks, you had enough time to have an affair with Hilda? Hilda?"

"An affair would be overstating it by half. More like a few dinners and two nights of sex. And yes, Hilda. What's wrong with Hilda? She's beautiful and smarter than me...well, almost. If Maggie and I hadn't gotten back together, Hilda and I might have really gone somewhere."

"Oh, no, sorry, you're right; she's a perfectly lovely woman and all. It's just...how can you have passionate 'on a break' sex with someone named Hilda? I just don't see it. Oh, Hilda, harder, Hilda, faster, Hilda. I can't see it. That would be like me trying to have really hot sex with some guy named Harold. Anyway, isn't she straight?"

"Oh, shut up. No, she's bisexual. I think I might have been her only. Beware the semester lesbian."

The agents drove ahead of Drew and Stephen this time and stopped a block away from the rundown white clapboard house. They found him hiding in the bathroom, cuffed him, and placed him in the back of the sedan. The whole transaction took less than ten minutes.

Back at headquarters, Baychamp produced the same lawyer Stephen and Drew had met earlier in P-Town. There would be no interview.

Chapter Twelve

J.J. was anxious to get the car back on time, Stephen was anxious to get back to more secure land-based phone lines in case Spree called back, and Drew was just anxious. They decided that if they left right away and ate diner on the fly, they could make it back to Provincetown before midnight. J.J., having performed her duty in driving them to Boston, took a well-earned nap in the backseat. Stephen was feeling fully a man behind the wheel of the Hummer. Chicken or no chicken, this was one powerful machine.

"Okay, so where does this leave us, Stephen? We have a dead woman, a dead dog belonging to the shooter's father, and a very expensive lawyer representing both of them. We have a set of witnesses, all of whom say the dog chased her into the bank."

"Maybe the dog was just tied up outside and got loose and it was just a coincidence that they were both going into the bank at the same time."

"I know, but who leaves a dog tied up all day at their job? I find that pretty unlikely."

"Or maybe she had drugs on her, and the dog got wind of it and started chasing her. I mean, it was a drug dog. Hey, what about that? Maybe she was a user." Stephen glanced in the rearview mirror to make sure J.J. was still down for the count.

"That's an interesting theory, but the tox screen came back negative."

"It was nine o'clock in the morning. Maybe she hadn't started in yet."

"Yeah, but that stuff stays in your system a long time. It would still have shown up on the tox screen."

"Maybe she was just holding. Maybe she was a dealer who didn't use."

"Ever heard of a dealer who didn't use?"

"Nope. Sure haven't." Stephen shifted hard into fourth gear. "So here we are back at square one."

"There has to be a missing piece, and we're running out of time. There still isn't anything here that makes this federal. If we don't figure this out soon, we're going to have to turn this over to the state police. Maybe there's something in the bank records. You did bring them, right?"

"Yes, of course, I did. They're right under the front seat. But we don't even know what we're looking for." Stephen kept one hand on the steering wheel and reached his hand down between Drew's legs and slid the briefcase out from underneath the passenger seat.

"I know it's a shot in the dark, but we have all this time before we get back and maybe we'll find something, I don't know, some pattern maybe. It's worth a try, it's not like I have anything else to do. Can you still drive if I pop on the interior light?"

"Yeah, it's fine. God I love this car it's *so...*"

"Macho?"

"Oh, yeah. Sure is. I must have one. It's so good for my self image. Minus the chicken, of course."

"To drive around D.C.? Why? So you can go to the Safeway in Dupont Circle without fear? You're too funny. By the way, did I miss any serious conversation between the two of you while I was sleeping before?" Drew began to sort the bank documents on her lap.

"A little. She really likes you, I think. As much as you can like someone you just met. Anyway, I like her. She meets the minimum standard."

"You have standards?" Drew looked up from the documents.

"I do for you."

Drew spent the next hour and a half combing through the bank records, hoping that some kind of pattern would emerge. The only ones that had appeared so far were deposits from local businesses—The Pied Piper, Spruce Up, and even Angel's. It was becoming increasingly difficult to concentrate on the records in the moving car. The road had taken on a shiny green-black slickness, and only a smattering of the braver stars had come out. The temperature had dropped back down to sweatshirt weather. Drew was fading fast. Stephen, on the other hand, was soaring on the adrenaline of the three hundred sixty horses at his fingertips and had failed to notice they hadn't bothered to stop for dinner.

"I know we need to get back, but if I don't get food soon, I'm not going to be able to concentrate long enough to finish this," Drew said. "Do you think there's anyplace at all to eat along this road? I know it's late."

"I'll start to look for signs. We could use some gas anyway."

"Big Bellies." The sound came from just over Drew's left shoulder.

"I beg your pardon?" Stephen glanced at the newly awake J.J. in the rearview mirror."

"Big Bellies. Two exits down. Better get off there, it's the only place I know of that's open all night. And, no, they don't have chicken Caesar salad or decaf lattés. I don't think they even serve decaf. You two will just have to cope," J.J. said in a sleepy voice with a mild overlay of annoyance at having been awakened.

"Oh, somebody woke up on the wrong side of the car, I see," Stephen said.

"So, solve the big mystery yet? Get your man and all that? Actually, we're pretty close to the tip of the Cape now; we might get there before eleven. Good god, how fast have you been going? Or have I been nodded off for several hours?"

"Both I'd say. But good news that we're close. Maybe we'll take the time to eat in. I could use the break," Drew said in the direction of the backseat.

"Yes, driving from the passenger seat can be exhausting, I'm sure," Stephen said in a voice that let Drew and J.J. know he wasn't happy to be sharing Drew's time with the doctor again.

"Okay, this is it."

"Yes, let's do eat in. We've bags of time now." J.J. stretched her arms their full length as she headed toward the entrance.

Big Bellies was truth in advertising. It was a fairly large restaurant for what was clearly a sixty- or seventy-year-old all-night diner. Its size was accentuated by the fact that only three other people were being served. They were sitting side by side on red vinyl stools at the long yellow Formica counter. All three were late middle-aged men, hunched over, drinking coffee from slightly chipped white porcelain mugs. It was hard to place who they might be or what might have brought them here at such a late hour. They were clearly locals, and it was too late for farmers or fishermen to be out.

Stephen steered Drew and J.J. to a table far from the mystery men.

They had expected an older waitress, hairnet hanging, dressed in a pink and white uniform reminiscent of a hospital candy striper, chewing gum thoughtlessly with dim teeth, and were startled when a beautiful late teenage girl appeared to take their order. "What will you all have?" she said in a quiet voice.

"Actually, could we get some menus first? Or is the menu on the wall somewhere?" Stephen looked around the restaurant, scanning the walls.

"This time of night, we only have pie. Blueberry or apple. And coffee, of course. But no decaf." The waitress continued to hold the pencil at the ready.

"Oh, okay. But could I get like a bagel instead? Something simple like that you might have left over from breakfast? It's so late for sugar," Drew said.

"We only have pie. Blueberry or apple. And only one or two blueberry slices left, so one has to choose apple. Good pie, though, you'll like it. We used to serve it with a money back guarantee, said if you don't like it, you get it for free. Then we had a bunch a lawyers come in here one time, and that was the end of that." The waitress smiled a little at the charm of her anecdote.

"Apple, blueberry, and blueberry then and coffee all around." Stephen pointed to each of them in turn as he called out the pie orders. "Oh, and some skim milk if you have it, otherwise just milk."

"Two blues, one apple, three coffees, and milk. Should be right out." The waitress actually wrote the order down in detail.

Stephen stretched out full length in the booth and leaned back against the inner wall. "I'm getting tired now, but wow, J.J., that's some car out there. I thought a car that big would be hard to handle, but it drives like a Beemer."

"I'm glad you like it. I find it quite silly really in that typically American way. You love your cars, the bigger the better. Everyone thinks it's the chicken that makes it look silly, but I rather think it has a silliness just of its own. What do you think, then?" J.J. directed the question to Drew, who was still reading the bank records now fanned out in front of her.

"What? Oh, the car. Yes, well, all I know is I could never drive it."

"So then you think it's silly, too?" J.J. said.

"No. I mean I could never actually drive it. As in drive it, drive it. It's like trying to maneuver a house. I don't know how you even keep it on the road. If I ever drove that up to a friend's house, I'd feel like I was invading them." Drew poured half of the tiny container of milk into the just-delivered coffee.

"That's right, J.J. We Americans are known for our fabulous cars. And you Brits are known for what again? Oh, Churchill and tea, that's right."

"Can't take a wee joke, then? All that bravado American hidden in that thin shell. I like the pastry by the way. Quite tasty," J.J. said to Drew.

"Oh, here you can have mine, too. Too late for pie for me. And could you let me out? I need to use the restroom big-time." Drew slid the pie sideways to J.J.

"It's not pastry, Doctor, it's pie. Pie. Pastry is totally different," Stephen said.

"Really? Very well then. You must explain the difference to me sometime. But I think I might use the loo myself before we go." J.J. slid out of the booth and headed in the same direction Drew had gone.

Drew was just opening the door of the bathroom to leave when J.J. gently pushed her back inside.

"In a hurry, then? Or time for a bit of a kiss?" J.J. slid her hands tightly around Drew's waist.

Drew kissed her hard on the mouth in lieu of an answer. Their movements were quick as boxers, jabbing and tugging at pieces of clothing while continuing to kiss so hard the scraping of teeth could be heard. In a few more movements, J.J. was pressing a now naked-to-the waist Drew face forward into the wall, biting the back of her neck in large mouthfuls and gently skimming her bare back with her fingernails. Cold tile. Warm Hands. Hot breath. A tongue. *God.* "J.J., I said no." *Did that come out or is it still in my head? Shallow breath. Breathe. God, that sound. So loud in my head. Is that my heart? God. Stop it. Stop it.*

The loud banging on the bathroom door went on for some time before it actually registered with them. Then they recognized Stephen's voice. "Drew. Drew, are you in there? Get out here now. This is important. I need to talk to you."

After a few moments of realignment and a few "just a minutes," and "I'll be right there," Drew opened the door. J.J. cast a steely glance at Stephen as she passed out of the door first. Once she did, Stephen rushed in and closed and locked the door behind him.

"You must be kidding me. In the bathroom? Please." Stephen stared at her.

"Have you gone completely over the top? I know we're under a lot of pressure,but stalking me in the bathroom is a bit much, even for you. And is there some reason you can't use the men's room?"

"Shit no. I didn't come in here for that. Listen to me now, this is serious. Like heart attack serious." Stephen reached over and turned the water in the sink faucet on full blast.

"My god. Someone had a heart attack. Oh, Stephen, not your mother. You poor thing."

"What? Oh, for crying out loud. No one had a heart attack. Besides, my mother will never be that courteous. She intends to linger for months. Listen to me. Spree called. We got a hit on the prints."

"Got a hit on Baychamp's prints? How is that possible?" Drew reached over with a puzzled look and turned off the water.

"No. Not Baychamp. The victim's prints." Stephen reached over and turned the water back on full blast. "Leave that on, it will muffle the sound. The Organized Crime Unit called. Are you ready for this? The dead woman in the bank is Sue Gambini."

"Who the hell is Sue Gambini?"

"As in Old Man Gambini. The Gambinis. East Coast crime family, New York, Jersey, Boston. Ringing any bells?"

"No. Why would it? I don't know anything about organized crime stuff. So Sue Gambini is his wife, I take it."

"No, his daughter,"

"His daughter? How old is this Gambini guy?"

"Well, apparently, he's older than dirt now. And cramming for finals big-time."

"Cramming for finals?" Drew said.

"Making amends, you know, before he goes to the big bocce ball game in the sky. He's been leaking like a sieve to OCU for months. The whole family's in witness protection."

"Since when? Wait a minute, are you telling me they think this was a mob hit? No way. Wait a minute. Remember I told you that J.J. said the suspect, well, victim now, I guess, had all that plastic surgery. That makes sense, doesn't it? They reconstructed her probably."

"Sort of, it wasn't exactly the focus of the story."

"So you're telling me that woozy little boy of a cop is a made guy? No way, I don't buy that."

"Made guy? I thought you didn't know about organized crime stuff."

"Hey, I watch *The Sopranos*. And I'll tell ya, little Billy Butthole is no Soprano. When do the OCU guys get here?"

"They're coming as soon as they can. Sooner than we would like, that's for sure."

"Okay, we're out of here." Drew rushed to the front of the restaurant, threw twenty dollars on the table, grabbed J.J. gently by the arm, and half-ran to the car. "J.J., can you drive us? I need

Stephen in the backseat. I know you aren't very fond of him at the moment, but he did the right thing in there. We need to get back to town right now. Could you do that for me without asking too much in return?" Drew scrambled into the backseat.

"Done then. Let's go." J.J. threw the Hummer into reverse.

"Okay, here's what we have now. Think, Stephen. Drug cop dad gives drug-sniffing dog to beat cop son. Dog and mob daughter get shot by cop son. Every witness says it's a clean shoot. Where's the missing piece?"

"Maybe the dad was into the mob for money. Maybe he sold them some drugs or stole some of their drugs. Some of those undercover guys lead pretty dodgy lives," Stephen said as he watched Drew speed read through the remaining bank records.

"Right. Right. Maybe so. But how did they know she would be at that bank at exactly that moment? The timing of this, if it was a hit, was pretty precise. This would have been pretty hard for even a pro to carry off, don't you think? It has to be in these records."

"Did you find anything? Should we both be looking? Might take less time that way and tick tock, tick tock."

"Nothing but deposits so far. There has to be more. Here, you take the withdrawals while I finish the deposits." Drew handed Stephen a thick stack of documents.

For the next half hour, they rode in silence except for the symphony of yawns and crinkling paper. Drew and J.J. shot occasional glances back and forth in the rearview, making a silent bargain about their unfinished business.

"We're about six miles out now. Just thought you might want to know," J.J. said over the backseat.

"Okay, thanks, honey." There was two seconds of silence followed by an audible intake of breath by Drew. J.J. tossed her head to the side and smiled in the rearview. Stephen looked at J.J., then at Drew, then at J.J., then at the still-gasping-for-breath Drew and mouthed "honey?" as a silent question. It hung suspended in the air the last six miles.

"Okay now. Back to business. There are only five deposits that match for individuals. All by electronic transfer. Let's see if we can match them with withdrawals. Let's look for Saturday's. Here's the list of names so far." Drew handed Stephen the short list of names she had culled from the deposit records, and he began scanning it with his fingers.

"Wait a minute. Bingo. What do you want to bet this is it? It has to be." Stephen pointed to the third name on the list.

"Nasus Gamble? What the hell kind of name is that?"

"Look, every Friday, an electronic transfer of exactly two thousand dollars. I betcha there are matching withdrawals every Saturday. Nasus, Drew, it's Susan spelled backward. And Gamble, either the FBI has a finely tuned sense of irony or she couldn't remember anything that wasn't as close as possible to her real last name. Look, the deposits are matching already, here are the first three, starting six months ago." Stephen handed Drew the deposit slips.

"Holy shit. That's it. Every Saturday at eight o'clock. But how did Billy Boy know that she came in there every Saturday? He's only been working at the bank a month or so. That's not enough time to plan a hit like this so precisely. Who signed the withdrawal slips? Go through them again."

"Shit, you're right, I think. They're almost all signed with the initials A.R."

"Hand me the personnel rosters. Here we go, Alexander Rodriguez."

"A.R., okay, where are your notes from the interviews?" Stephen passed Drew his spiral bound witness notebook, and she began furiously flipping the pages. Finally, her finger came to rest on the name. "That little mother fucking sack of shit. It's Mango."

"Mango? Mango is a mob guy? Isn't that like Don Corleone handing the family over to Fredo instead of Michael?"

"No, he's not a mob guy. No mos in the mob. He's probably a druggie. They probably bought his skinny little skeevy lyin' ass for a few bags of good coke. Let's go."

"Go? As in out? We're still driving, you might notice."

"Oh, right. Good point. Honey, can you drop us back at Angel's? We still have some work to do tonight, I'm afraid." Drew turned to Stephen and mouthed the words, "Shit. Stop me."

"Sure, love. And I will see you...?"

"Uh, well, that depends on how long this takes. But definitely breakfast. I mean, if you're free, that is. Didn't mean to presume that you would be." Drew began stuffing the loose documents back into her briefcase.

"I might be seeing patients then. Office hours. Unless you come by before six for some scramble." J.J. pulled up into the driveway of Angel's and killed the engine.

"Scramble it is." Drew leapt out of the door.

"Okay, Stephen, let's go."

"Go? As in out? Now?" Stephen stood, arms akimbo, by the front gate to Angel's.

"Funny. Yes, as in let's go out and find this sack of shit, so we can find out what happened. You do remember that's what we do."

"You're nuts. I'm not going out chasing some mob guy. Let OCU handle it when they get here."

"Fine, I'll do it myself." Drew handed him her briefcase and headed down the street.

Chapter Thirteen

Stephen ran back to the room, dropped the briefcases, and started out after Drew. He caught up with her after a few blocks. "Okay, Xena Warrior Princess, where do we start?"

"I don't know. But this town is so small. I'll look in every bar if I have to. And I still prefer Wonder Woman; it's the pointed bra fetish. I've loved her since I was eight. But first I want to reinterview Mr. and Mrs. Elvis."

"Because we didn't make enough fun of them the first time?"

"No. He was the most adamant about the fact the victim had screamed, 'money, money,' when she ran into the bank. His testimony supports the foiled robbery theory. We have to nail that down, don't you think?"

"Yep, we do."

The Carnival atmosphere was in full swing again, and Commercial Street was swarming with shirtless young men, their tanned, perfectly formed chests glowing with strands of brightly colored beads, their rounded muscled bottoms barely covered in little more than a variety of expensive underwear.

"What is it with you guys and this running around in your underpants thing anyway? Does it always have to be hanging right out there? Have you no sense of mystery?"

"Yes, you've hit on exactly what gay men crave. Mystery. And you should talk, Ms. Sex in the Bathroom."

"We did not have sex in the bathroom. Women, I assure you, do not have sex in the bathroom. There was hardly enough room in there for me to have sex with myself, much less someone else."

"Masturbation comes up so rarely in conversation; I don't know how to respond to that. Go team? And all I know is, I saw what I saw."

"For two women to have sex in the bathroom, it would take like an hour and a half. The lines in the women's room are long enough without that."

"An hour and a half? Good god, why so long?"

"The vagina is a lot more complicated than it appears at first glance. There's just a lot goin' on in there. It takes patience, and timing is everything."

"Okay, okay, that's all I need to know. I don't need my own private vagina monologue."

"Come on, this is the address they gave us."

Mr. and Mrs. Elvis were packing to leave on the morning Cape Air flight as Stephen and Drew arrived at the Well Wisher Inn at the far east end of town. The queen-sized bed in their room was strewn with plaid shirts and several sets of colorful salt and pepper shakers.

"We have a real nice collection back home. Got 'em all set out real pretty in a glass case. Right next to all our Elvis pieces. They make a nice accent." Mrs. Butler held up a matching pair shaped like a pickle and an olive. "These are summer ones."

"Going somewhere?" Drew closed the door to the room behind her.

They were not fleeing the jurisdiction after all, just pre-packing to see what they might have to ship home. They stuck pretty much to their original stories. Mrs. Butler had nothing to add and sat in the side chair, looking at her husband and stroking the plastic shakers for comfort. Mr. Butler remained adamant that he had nothing to add to his previous renderings of events. He said he could have been wrong about the "money, money" part of the story, but he really didn't think so. That was just how he remembered it.

Drew and Stephen made their way through the barely lit side

streets back to Commercial.

"Man, those two are totally GPRP. Don't we think?" Stephen said, laughing.

"GPRP?"

"Gene Pool Reclamation Project."

"They're just two nice people. Just two nice people. Quirky maybe, I'll give you that."

"Quirky indeed."

"Sometimes people invent quirky. To prevent themselves from dying of boredom. I mean, how much salt and pepper do you think one couple can consume? They're just trying to find something interesting about themselves. Just like the rest of us. Besides, somebody has to be the reason we still need directions on the shampoo bottle."

"Thank god. For a minute there, you sounded like you were channeling Maggie."

"Don't even start that with me. I'm hanging by a thread here, and you know how well I sew."

"You asked me to help you stop yourself. Remember?"

"Yes, I'm sorry. I did. Thank god you came in that bathroom when you did."

"I knew it!"

"I'm telling you, five more minutes pinned up against that wall, and I would have given that woman everything, including my car."

"The Porsche?"

"Well, okay, my old car. But still."

Two very large, very hairy drag queens, one dressed as a princess and one as a pea, passed them going the opposite direction. As they did, the princess reached out and hung a double strand of walnut-sized white faux pearls around Stephen's neck and patted his chest gently. "There ya go, honey, now you're Barbara Bush."

"So that's what they mean by 'Pearls before swine,'" Stephen countered.

An increasing number of drag queens began passing them on the street. There were multiple Marilyns, Chers, Barbras, a few

Madonnas—the religious and pop versions—and even one Rosie O'Donnell. As they passed, they would occasionally toss their Carnival beads to Stephen, who, not wanting to spoil his classic Barbara Bush look, would drop them around Drew's neck.

"They do Rosie as drag now? Where are all these guys going? Is there like a drag queen convention or something? They're all going the other way."

"I don't know. Should we ask them? Here, wait." Stephen walked across the street to two men in blond wigs with black plastic birds coming out in all directions. Each was dressed in a tan woman's suit from the forties with fake blood smeared everywhere. "Okay, I give up, what are you guys dressed as?"

"Tippi Hedrens, of course. Silly boy. Silly cute top boy. My, aren't we young and gorgeous," Tippi one said.

"Actually, honey, I think the plural is Tippis Hedren. You know, like Bettes Davis or attorneys general," said Tippi two.

"And what can we do for you, gorgeous one? You into birds or blonds? We don't do three-ways," said Tippi number one.

"But we do do two-ways twice," said Tippi two.

"As appealing as that is, I just want to know where you're going."

"To heaven and back if you want, honey."

"Or to hell in a hand basket."

"How is Helena Handbasket? I haven't seen that girl all season," Tippi one asked.

"She's in Jersey, honey, her mother is sick."

"So what's it gonna be, gorgeous boy? Heaven or hell?" said Tippi one.

"Actually, I really just wanted to know where you were going. I mean, as in right now. You girls all seemed to be headed in the same direction."

"The wrong direction, if ya ask me," said Tippi two.

"Okay, bird boys, the question is, where are you going right now? Where are all of you going? What is over that way?" Drew pointed down the street.

"Ooh. Okay, Melissa Etheridge Xena Warrior Princess, calm down."

"She prefers Wonder Woman," Stephen said.

"Oh, us too. We love that pointed bra thing she has going on. You could put your eye out."

"And you're going where?" Drew said.

"Oh, sorry. It's drag bingo night."

"Where?"

"At the church down the way a few blocks. Just follow the sound of clicking heels."

Drew grabbed Stephen by the arm and swept him down the street. They wove in and out of drag queens from every era. Jane Mansfields, Joan Crawfords (with coat hangers, and from the Baby Jane era because a classic never goes out of style), Bettes Davis, Dianas (royal and pop), Judys, Lizas, and Lornas (there's always a newbie), even one lone Celine Dion (gagged, of course). "Geez. Look at this, Stephen, there's like a million of them. It's like a drag queen hall of mirrors."

"Really. Who let the dogs out?"

The lawn in front of the church was crammed end to end with picnic tables. It was a sea of wigs and huge hats. Down the long entrance at the front of the church was a small stage. "B as in Best In Show seven. I as in I am and you're not twenty-two. O as in Oh, shit." Mango dropped the microphone and took off running.

Stephen and Drew ran after him. Stephen chased him across the yard and past the church. Drew circled around the back of the theater next door. As Mango came around the corner, Drew used the only weapon she had and threw the fist full of Carnival beads on the ground. Mango started in a slow slide, then tumbled over and over onto the grass. Drew stood over him.

"Get up you lying bucket of fuck. We know everything." As Mango stood, he lunged his left foot forward and dug his heel into the top of Drew's foot, breaking skin. A few moments later, Stephen rounded the corner and found her, heaped on the ground, bleeding and mumbling, "you little skeeving motherfucker."

Chapter Fourteen

"I'm telling you, Stephen, when they find that guy, he's a dead man." Drew lay in the hammock, her wounded foot elevated, covered with a bag of frozen peas.

"Well, first, they have to find him. I think the odds of that are pretty small. He could be anywhere. Here, let me get some real ice for that, you look awful. Where is Captain Underpants anyway? I thought she'd be here by now with the pain pills."

"Don't bother, it's fine. Do I look as stupid as I feel right now?"

"Pretty much, yeah." Stephen handed her a cup of coffee with a straw so she could drink it without sitting up. "Careful, this is still pretty hot. What the hell were you thinking doing that? You're not a cop. You do know that. He could really have hurt you. I mean in a seriously grim way. Please promise me you won't ever do that again."

"Yeah, okay. But could you save the lecture until I'm feeling a little better? Damn, where is she? I could really use something more than Advil here."

"Don't know. Her office said she was on a call or something and she would be here as soon as possible."

"Oh, did you talk to that little baby dyke that we met over there, her receptionist? I don't think she likes me. Maybe she never gave her the message. Goddamn this hurts."

"You know I could just go take a stroll underneath the docks and see what comes of it."

"Stephen, could you? Could you go out and commit a felony for me because my foot hurts?"

Stephen rose to go. "Sit down, you crazy person. Besides, physical pain is kind of a welcome change in a way. It hurts like hell, but ultimately, you know it'll heal. The only unknown being the length of the scar."

"Now who's Rita Hayworth? Aren't you in too much pain for analogy?"

Drew laughed. "Shut up. Yeah, actually I am."

"As long as we have some downtime here. Do tell, Mother, what are you going to do about the doctor?" Stephen arched an eyebrow.

"Go away."

"No."

"I can't answer that."

"I don't understand why you won't let yourself have this. Don't you think you've been on punishment long enough?" Stephen crossed his arms over his chest.

"I don't know, I just can't. I can get right to the tipping point but no farther. I guess it feels like cheating. I can't do that to Maggie, to us. It feels disloyal."

"Well, apparently, you didn't have any problem humping Hilda. So what's the difference?"

"Oh, how did I just know Hilda would come up again? You really are mad that I never told you about that, aren't you? Hilda? I was twenty-something then, Stephen. Hilda was a nothing, a hiccup, akin to having lunch. Just something you need to do in the course of an average day."

"Yes, I'm still mad. I can't believe I didn't know about Hilda. So why can't J.J. just be lunch?"

"Because she isn't. When she's around, I feel like I'm living in the space between words. Turn my head to the left, I see what has come before, to the right I can't quite see what's coming. It's paralyzing."

"So you're like a punctuation mark?"

"Shut up." Drew threw her straw in Stephen's direction. "It

just feels wrong, that's all I know."

"But is she funny?"

"Yes. Fuck. Yes, she's funny. She is funny. Annoyingly so. Smart funny."

"That bitch."

"I know. Didn't god give this girl enough with the brains and the beauty? She has to be funny, too? Can she leave nothing for the regular girls?"

"So what's the problem again?"

"Have you heard nothing I've said?" Drew propped herself up on her elbows and stared at him.

"For crying out loud. She's gone, Drew. Maggie is not here."

"I know she's not here." Drew waved her arm in front of her. "But she's still here." Drew pointed to her head, then her heart.

"Oh, well, that's a problem then." Stephen took the empty coffee cup from her hand and set it on the table.

"I wish I could just do it, the—almost, sort of—is making me feel like my hair's on fire all the time. It's crowding out other things. Every time I get within a foot of her, I feel like I'm two seconds away from breaking the Girlfriend Rule."

"The Girlfriend Rule?"

"You break it, you bought it."

"Captain Underpants seems pretty sturdy to me. So I wouldn't worry about it."

"It's not her I'm worried about."

Chapter Fifteen

"'New blue' Choo shoe lone clue."

Stephen was convinced that would be the headline in Friday's *Provincetown Banner*, as he and Drew stood staring at the body. Mango was lying face up on the ground with a five-inch high heel firmly imbedded in his jugular vein. Blood was spattered in a three-foot circle around him, and a larger, thickening stream of blood mapped its way down Bradford Street. The local police held back the crowd of onlookers.

"But the shoe looks black, Stephen, at least in this light. With all this blood, it's hard to tell." Drew bent as close to the body as she could without losing her balance.

"Black *is* the new blue. So it definitely works." Stephen peered over Drew's shoulder. "Damn, sister, that's a honkin' lotta blood."

"I know. It hit the jugular. Gotta expect that, I guess. I thought it was the other way around. I thought blue was the new black." Drew straightened up and stretched her lower back, put her hand on Stephen's shoulder, and lifted her injured foot.

"Only if you count the spring of ninety-nine. Here, lean on me. We need to get you off that foot." Stephen attempted to guide Drew over to one of the police cars.

"No, wait. I want to walk the blood line." With Stephen's help, Drew hobbled along, following the rivulet of thinning blood for more than half a block, until it pooled around a crushed cigarette package and turned back on itself.

"Jesus, Mary, and Joseph, I'll be surprised if there's any blood left in this guy at all." Drew balanced against Stephen. "I feel kind of bad now, saying next time I see him, he's going to be a dead man."

"Really. Who's in charge of irony anyway? I want to meet them. Come on now, you really need to sit down." Stephen helped Drew over to Chief Santora's unmarked blue sedan and deposited her sideways on the front seat.

"What do we have so far? Anything?" Drew said to Santora.

"Not much. They're still canvassing the witnesses, but nobody seems to have seen anything until that guy was walking his dogs and came across the body. He called it in about five a.m." Santora pointed to a middle-aged man in an expensive striped polo shirt holding the faux diamond-studded leashes of two aged dachshunds. "Are you going to wait here for the coroner? It could take awhile; he's got a bit of a drive and he just came in last night from his month at Mass. General ."

"Yes. If you don't mind, I think we'll wait. The body can't be moved until the agents get here anyway, and I'd like to get my hands on that shoe as soon as possible. We don't have to take up your car, though. We'll set up shop across the street. Let me know if anything else comes from the canvass, and if you could leave some guys behind for crowd control until my guys get here, that would be great."

"No problem. What'd ya do to that foot anyway?" Santora pointed down at Drew's badly swollen foot.

"High heels. She's not used to them. I tried to tell her, but you know how women are." Stephen scooped Drew out of the car and walked her across the street to The New Café.

The café had just opened, and they were the only people in the place other than the two young sleepy-looking Hispanic waitresses. They settled themselves in the front booth that looked directly across the street to where the body lay. "So did we totally screw this up, or what? I'm in so much trouble."

"Yeah. We're pretty much screwed on this deal. So? How do we save this? It has to be a mob hit." Stephen ordered coffee for both of them.

"Yeah, it seems like it would be. It must have leaked in Boston after the arrest. But that seems funny to me. That doesn't leave much time between then and this. They couldn't have driven down in time. Cape Air. We should have somebody check the passenger lists."

Drew propped her leg up on the seat across from her.

"Yes, I'm sure they gave their actual names."

"It's really hard to fly now without proper ID. Does that sound stupid? I think I'm in over my head on this mob stuff. This is really not our area. Maybe it's time we confess error and turn this whole thing over to OCU in Boston. Geez, this is like the worst coffee I've ever had." Drew slid the coffee cup away from her. "I feel nauseous. Maybe I should eat something."

"I don't know what we should do, but we for sure can't do that. Those guys from Boston will screw us so bad with the front office in D.C. that we'll both end up permanently in the Freedom of Information Office. I don't know about you, but I'm not prepared for a life of indexing and collating. Here, eat the other half of this." Stephen slid the uneaten half of his bagel in her direction. "Buck up, soldier, we need a plan."

"Right now, I'd settle for four Advil. But you're right, of course. We need to dig our way back out of this hole. You know we don't really know anything about this guy. Let's start with a search of his apartment. We need a warrant." Drew shifted in her seat.

"What do we need a warrant for? The guy's dead. I'm going to get you some Advil."

"I know, but just out of an abundance of caution. We don't have to go back to Boston. The local prosecutor should be able to get it for us. Then let's start back at that bar where he did his show. See what we can shake loose. I don't think the pharmacy will be open yet. Where's the damn coroner anyway?"

"Why is that? Why isn't Austin doing it? What happened to her anyway? First, she's a no-show yesterday and now she's a no-show here. Did you chase her off or something? I'm going to check the pharmacy. If it's closed, I'll find something else. You look like you're ready to heave."

"I might just actually. No, I didn't chase her off. Funny. Like I have that power. But I didn't have them call her, either. This is getting complicated enough. Plus, she's fully compromised now as a witness for us. I don't think she could even be presented to the grand jury at this point."

"Yeah, that's right on. I'm going." Stephen turned to go and came face to face with Dr. Austin. "Oh, speak of the devil."

"Am I?" Dr. Austin stepped around Stephen and slid into the booth next to Drew's foot. "It's clear from the look of you, you're not made for morning."

Drew smiled sheepishly. "Good morning, Doctor. Stop to see our boy over there?"

"Couldn't get too close, but, yes, looks like he was hit with some sort of object or something, is it? So that's something to do with your mystery? What's this then? This the injury your Stephen called about?" Dr. Austin bent down to get a closer look at Drew's foot.

"Oh, yeah. Hurts like hell, actually. I'm afraid it might be getting infected. Yes, he was killed by a high heel, at least we think so. Same thing that caused that. Well, not the same shoe exactly. Not that we know of. That would be too creepy. So, an infection? I'm really having trouble walking on it. I thought that might get better when the swelling went down, but it hasn't. Permanently damaged, am I?"

"Might be just the beginning of an infection. I'll write you a script for that. I'm a little more worried it might be broken. Can't tell yet. Feet are hard in that way, not like there's much you can do about it anyway. Might try wrapping it for you, might help to have a wee bit more support than you have now. I'd tell you to stay off it, but from what I've seen, you don't seem to ever stop moving. Permanent damage? That seems fanciful. But I'll give you something to deal temporarily with the pain. Only take it before sleep, though, they'll make you a bit blurry."

"Blurry sounds pretty good right now. Maybe I'll finally get some sleep."

"Careful with that, they may give you dreams you'll bring

back with you. I've a few wounded tourists waiting for me, I'm afraid." Dr. Austin reached down and gently kissed Drew on the big toe. "There we are then. Come by my office when you have a moment between mysteries and I'll wrap her up for you."

Stephen whisked by J.J. as she was leaving the café. He set the bag from the pharmacy down on the table and slid in next to Drew.

"All better now that we've seen the doctor?"

"Shut up. Did you get my Advil or what?"

"Right here, the giant king-sized bottle. I think the kid behind the counter thought I had the hangover of all time." Stephen unscrewed the cap, broke the seal on the bottle, spilled out four Advil, and handed them to Drew, along with what water was left in the only remaining glass on the table. "Here, take this before you pass out."

"Thanks, and I'm not going to pass out. I'm way too pissed off for that." Drew threw the Advil into the back of her throat and gulped the water in two seconds. "Here, she gave me these, too. I think one is for a cream, and the other for codeine."

"Mmm, tasty." Stephen slipped the prescription in his shirt pocket.

"She said only to take it at night. Of course, then she said if I did take it at night, it would probably give me bad dreams. My life continues to be filled with nothing but good choices."

"Isn't that what we're having right now? What else did she say?" Stephen threw ten on the table and helped Drew to her feet.

"She told me to come to see her between mysteries. And then she kissed my big toe."

"Oh, you must have shown her your copy of the Constitution. That always makes 'em hot." Stephen laughed.

"Shut up. You laugh, but some of the best sex I've ever had started with a heated discussion of the First Amendment and Thomas Paine's view of secular humanism. I'd tell you to try it, but I don't know if it works as well on boys."

"You are a complete freak."

"Oh, I know it. Come on, let's go get a warrant."

The local assistant prosecutor looked like he was twenty-two and sounded like he was twelve still undergoing the voice change of a confused choir boy. He either had never drafted a warrant before or was just being a jerk. Drew and Stephen couldn't quite tell. Finally, they convinced him to get his supervisor.

"Is this guy just a total dick or what?" Stephen was tapping his foot madly on the yellow linoleum tile.

"Really. It's just a simple search warrant for this guy's apartment. What's the deal? Why is everything with you people always a dick-measuring contest anyway?"

"You people? Don't lump me in with that guy. We're not a society of one. How would you like it if I lumped you in with Suzanne Somers?"

"Ewww. Point taken. Where is this guy, for crying out loud? We're losing time here."

Twenty minutes later, the assistant prosecutor emerged with the typed warrant and gave Drew and Stephen directions to the courthouse.

"Here, the judge will meet you in chambers. I've already spoken to her. She's expecting you."

"Thanks. And let me guess, first in your class at Harvard Law, were you?" Stephen slipped the warrant into his briefcase.

"Fuck you. You people from Washington are all the same." The prosecutor started waving his finger in Stephen's face.

"Well, if you mean smart, then you're right. And fuck you, too, you passive aggressive little shit." Stephen took a step forward.

"Oh, that's nice. And after all the help I just gave you."

Drew stepped between them. "Actually, it is nice. 'Fuck you' is Gaelic for 'Have a nice day,' Come on, Stephen. We're done here."

Chapter Sixteen

"Why does murder always make me hungry?" Drew was running her fingers over the spines of the paperback books stuffed into Mango's six-foot-tall bookshelf. It was one of the few pieces of furniture in the tiny apartment. Local police officers had cordoned off the apartment and were sweeping the bedroom for anything that looked like a clue. "I don't see anything here out of the ordinary. But I don't want to rush. Maybe we should eat lunch and come back."

"On the upside, there isn't that much more to go through. On the downside, this guy seemed to love only two things: porn and bingo." Stephen emerged from behind the sofa bed, balancing a tall set of boxes. "Look at this shit, there's like twenty bingo games here. And this is only half of what's back there. What's up with that?"

"I don't know. Maybe he was on a bingo team." Drew started opening the boxes one by one. "Or maybe this is his stash hideaway. Maybe there's drugs in here."

"You don't play bingo in teams. Haven't you ever played bingo?"

"No, I don't think so. If I have, I don't remember it." Drew opened the first box a little too quickly, causing a spill of colorful translucent round disks to scatter across the coffee table and onto the floor. She picked one up and held it to the light. "What the hell are these things for?"

Stephen took it from her fingers. "That's how you play. Someone calls a letter and a number, and if you have it on your card, you put this over it, like this." Stephen drew out one of the small yellowed bingo cards and set it on the table and placed the dot over B6. If you get a line across, then you have bingo."

"This is fun? This had to be invented by a straight person living in Idaho." A police officer stuck his head around the corner of the bedroom.

"What do you want us to do with all these shoes in here? They're mostly ladies shoes, but there's a ton of them."

Drew rose, walked to the bedroom, and scanned a giant pile of high heels that were heaped in the bottom of the tiny closet.

"I hate to say this, guys, but we probably need to bag and tag them all, given how this happened. If you find any that don't have matches, tag those red. We still don't know if it was his shoe or somebody else's that, well, you know. And I don't need to tell you we need the computer and any and every disk you find."

"What about all this porn? And all these games and stuff up here." The officer pointed to a shelf high up in the closet. It was stacked as far as you could see with porno tapes and bingo games.

"Good Lord, there's more of them? Oh, great. Yes, all of it. Bag and tag. We're going to finish up in here, then head down to the coroner's office. We'll leave the stuff we want on the coffee table. I can't thank you enough. We'll swing back by the station when we're done with the body."

Stephen was still sitting in front of the coffee table, examining the stack of boxes. "This is really weird. Maybe he's one of those eBay freaks who collect weird shit. Nice taste in porno, though. Some of these are classics." Drew sat next to Stephen.

"There's like fifty more of these in there. More porn, too. And I'm sure he spent all his time wondering why he couldn't get a boyfriend." Drew began picking up the boxes and looking underneath each one. "You know some of these are really old, this one is like from 1964. Maybe they're worth some money. Is there money in bingo?"

"There certainly has been for the Catholic Church." Stephen stood and stretched. "I can't understand how you got through all that Catholic schooling without once playing bingo." He helped Drew to her feet.

"You might have noticed, I'm not much of a joiner. Come on, let's stack this stuff, then we need to see how the coroner's coming along. I want to see that shoe. But can we stop at Dr. Austin's on the way? This thing is really killing me now. No pun intended."

"Yes. For once, I think you're seeing the doctor is a good idea."

They opted for a cab, even though Austin's office was only seven blocks away. The waiting room was overflowing with exhausted-looking white people with small snot-dribbling children crawling over them crying in fits and starts. One older man held a shoebox in his lap that appeared to move periodically on its own.

"Oh, great. Come on. Stephen, let's go. This is going to take forever. Plus, who knows what we'll catch if we stay in here."

"This is a true glimpse into the dark side. We aren't leaving yet. Let me see if I can bribe the little baby dyke into finding Austin." Stephen maneuvered his way carefully through the growing growling hive of children on the floor over to the reception desk. He didn't even get to open his mouth. The receptionist looked around him to where Drew was standing leaned against the wall.

"Go get her. The doctor is expecting her. I have a room waiting."

Drew and Stephen settled in the small examination room. He sat squeezed into a small faux green leather chair with wooden arms, and Drew sat on the examination table, her back propped against the wall, her foot sticking straight out in front of her. She glanced to the left, and when she saw the glint of light spark off the stirrups sticking out of the end of the table, she laughed out loud so hard, she toppled over and had to right herself. "Good god. She's too much. Really. Ow, that makes my stomach hurt."

The sound of Drew's laugh made Stephen laugh, too, even though he had no idea what was so funny. "What? What's so funny?"

"Uh, never mind. You don't want to know."

"What? Tell me. I haven't heard you laugh that loud in a long time. You didn't take that medication already, did you?"

"What? No." Drew's laughter had begun to subside. "Let's just say it's a girl thing and leave it at that." The receptionist knocked, then popped her head in the door to let them know that Dr. Austin would be there in a few minutes. As she did, she walked over to the end of the table, removed the stirrups from their storage place, brought them up, and locked them into place. She walked across the room, grabbed a stack of eight-by-eleven gauze pads, ripped open their packages, walked backed over, and stacked them in a neat cradle in the exposed stirrups. She closed the door gently behind her.

"She's a model of efficiency, that girl. A creepy model of efficiency. What are these for anyway?" Stephen bent over and began inspecting the stirrups.

"She must be kidding." Drew began to laugh again, this time so hard it drew small tears into the corner of her eyes. "Ow, I really have to stop doing that. My stomach is starting to hurt worse than my foot. I think I need some food. And don't play with those. You don't even know how sorry you'll be."

"What's so goddamn funny?" Stephen inched away from the stirrups. "Why? What is it?"

"Okay, you know when you take your car in for repair."

"Yeah. I don't actually have a car, but yeah, and?"

"And they hoist it up on that pneumatic thing so they can see underneath it?"

"Yeah. And?"

"Well, it's sorta like that, only for women. You know, for when women come in for their thirty thousand-mile checkup. Get it?"

Stephen stood staring at the stirrup, then at Drew with a puzzled look on his face. "Uh…oh! It's the thing with the thing where you do the…oh. Wow. That seems so eighteenth century. Isn't that uncomfortable? Get down, I want to see."

"What? I will not."

"Come on, it's the only chance I'll ever get." The gentle

knock at the door prompted Stephen to retake his seat. The broad smile on Dr. Austin's face could not quite hide the tired look in her eyes.

"Sorry for the delay, it's stacks on out there, appears every child in town has the beginnings of the flu today." Dr. Austin placed her hand on Drew's knee. "How's it feeling now? Better or worse? Still looks quite swollen."

"Actually, it hurts like hell."

"Let's see if we can help that a bit. I'll let you take the shoe and sock off." Dr. Austin shuttled past Stephen over to the small counter. She opened the drawer and withdrew a pair of rubber gloves, a white plastic tube, a tan Ace bandage, and a large round glass object. She walked back over to the examining table and placed the objects on a steel tray. "We need to lie still for this." Dr. Austin placed her hands on each of Drew's shoulders and laid her down face up on the table. She placed Drew's feet one by one in the stirrups and bent down to examine her injured foot. "Wicked."

"I beg your pardon?"

"Looks wicked." Dr. Austin picked up the large round glass object and placed it in front of her face. It appeared to be a magnifying glass. "I think now that the shoe's off, it's bound to swell more. But I don't see any debris, so that lowers the chance there's an infection rooting around in there. But let's not take any chances, you don't seem the innately lucky sort."

Drew laughed at that. The doctor picked up the rubber gloves and slid one on to each hand. She picked up the white tube, unscrewed the cap, and pinched out a large amount of white cream. She turned the stirrup holding Drew's good leg as far away as it would go. This increased by half the awkwardness of Drew's already awkward position. Stephen looked at Drew, who looked at Stephen, who looked at the doctor, who looked at Drew, who looked at Stephen, who looked at the doctor.

Dr. Austin smiled a little. "That's a fanciful notion you're both having. It's antibiotic cream. Might be a wee bit cold to the touch. Prepare yourself." Drew winced a little as the cream was applied. Dr. Austin then wrapped the foot in a firm but comforting series of crisscrossing Xs. There was half a knock at the door, and the receptionist's head appeared briefly. The entire left side of her hair was dotted with brightly colored pieces of what must have been, at some point, whole pieces of cereal.

"Sorry to interrupt, Dr. Austin. But they're getting out of control out here. It's puke city."

"Oh, sorry then to abandon you. I'll be right to it." Dr. Austin looked at Drew and smiled. "Okay, you're done for now. I'll do a more thorough examination later."

Chapter Seventeen

The coroner looked like a homeless 1940s movie star. His chiseled scruffy face was the map of Ireland. Drew thought he seemed way too young to be in this business. In her experience, the grim task of puzzling out death had always been the business of aging men well on their way to approaching their own outer boundary. His youth and beauty were a little startling. He introduced himself as Dr. Colin R. Falon. Emphasizing the "R," as if he had often been confused with some other young beautiful Irish coroner also named Colin Falon.

"Stephen Shaunessey. And this is Drew Morgan." Stephen almost stepped on Drew's good foot as he cut in front of her during the introduction. After several minutes of overly long handshaking and a puffy introduction by Stephen of their purpose, Dr. Falon led them down a long narrow hallway.

"I usually ask people if they're ready before I open the door. Give them a moment to collect themselves. I suppose I don't need to do that with the two of you. But it's a bit of a habit, I'm afraid."

"Yes, I understand. You are in a tough business. But we're ready." Drew nodded in the direction of the steel door.

The body was laid out on a broad steel table and was covered head to toe in an army green sheet that carried the sheen of clear fluid. A gray steel gurney sat empty in the middle of the room. The light was blindingly white. The three of them approached the table together.

"So what can you tell us?" Drew looked at Falon.

"I'll show you the wound if you want, but it's pretty gruesome. I'm not quite done with it yet. It's quite deep. If the larynx hadn't caught just the tip of it, it might have gone almost all the way through." Dr. Falon showed the entry of the shoe on his own throat.

"So he died from the wound or the massive blood loss?" Stephen walked over next to Falon to get a closer look.

"Neither. Actually, the blood loss wasn't as bad as it looked out there."

"It wasn't? How is that possible with a wound like that?" Drew said.

"I think once it was wedged in his throat, the shoe may have acted as somewhat of a plug, if that's the right word. The blood loss was significant, but it was more likely that the airway became constricted. He more likely died of asphyxiation. As I said, I'm not quite through yet. And given that the heel was made of metal, I wouldn't rule out blood loss quite yet."

"Metal? I'm going to want to see that. But first, can you show me the angle of entry. Was it left to right or right to left?" Drew looked closely at the doctor's throat as he took a pen from his pocket and pointed it straight at his throat.

"Neither. It was dead on straight. Almost surgical in its precision. The odds of it happening while he was still moving are almost incalculably low."

"Even if it was done by a pro?" Stephen kept his eyes on the point of the pen still pointed at the doctor's throat.

"A pro? What do you mean by that?"

"He means a person hired to kill this guy. A professional killer." Dr. Falon replaced the pen in his pocket and looked at Drew as if she were giving him an unannounced quiz in which he had to name all the U.S. presidents in reverse order. "A hit man, Doctor. A hit man. We think that's a distinct possibility in this case."

"Oh. That never...a hit man? That never would have entered my mind. A hit man on Cape Cod? Seems impossible. I'll have to think about that. I don't really know how to answer that question. But as you suggest, I will retrace my steps a little bit, then do the rest of the autopsy with that in mind."

"That would be good. In the meantime, I'd really like to see that shoe."

Dr. Falon took them to a small back room that was filled floor to ceiling with white cardboard boxes, stacked and indexed in some manner. In the center of the room sat a small black steel desk. In the center of the desk was the shoe wrapped in plastic. It had not yet been bagged. Stephen reached toward it. "No, wait, Stephen, we'll screw up the chain of evidence."

"Right," Stephen said.

"Doctor, can you remove that from the plastic and see if we can identify the make and model?"

"Make and model? It's not a car. She means designer and the catalog number and, of course, the size and width." Dr. Falon carefully unwrapped the shoe and turned it upside down. "See, Drew, I told you it was black." He scribbled the information on a small white pad on his desk and handed it to Stephen. Drew peered over the doctor's shoulder to get a closer look at the heel.

"Wow, it really narrows, doesn't it? That's no bigger around than a pencil. Stephen, take a few pictures of this." Dr. Falon replaced the shoe and led Drew and Stephen back to the front door.

"By the way, he didn't have any other wounds, did he?" Drew said.

"Not that I've seen so far, no."

"Evidence of drugs? On the body or in the tox screen?"

"The tox screen is still pending. I don't usually look for body evidence unless something comes up positive like heroin. But I'll make an exception."

"We appreciate that. Please call us as soon as you have more information."

They waited ten minutes for the cab they had taken to Barnstable to return to pick them up for the return trip. Stephen sat on one end of a long wooden bench and motioned for Drew to join him. He raised her leg and placed her damaged foot on his thigh and began to massage her toes one by one. Drew lay flat on the bench with her hands behind her head. She closed her eyes to shield them from the sun.

"Geez, is that guy gorgeous or what?" Stephen continued massaging.

"Yeah, he really is. Unnervingly so. Almost creepy. That feels great."

"Creepy? Creepy how? I think you need more blood circulation in this thing."

"The contrast of beauty and death. That's, I don't know, like saying blood and candy. It just instantly loses its appeal. Like if you found out Allison Janney was secretly a serial killer or something. I know, I think I need more ice on it. Maybe when we get back."

"Allison who? Maybe I should run over to that gas station and see if they have ice right now. Your foot actually seems warm to me."

"CJ from 'The West Wing.'"

"Oh, your TV girlfriend. Yes, I remember now. I don't care what you say, that guy is too gorgeous, even if he does play with dead bodies for a living. Besides, I didn't see that blood and candy thing, which I must say is a disgusting image, slowing you down any with Dr. Austin, now did I?"

"Well, that's true."

"Why is the Cape so crawling with Irishers anyway? I thought this was founded by a bunch of Methodists or something."

"It's close to Boston, remember? I think that ice might be a good idea actually, if you don't mind. If the cab comes, I'll just make him wait. Could you?"

"Yep. Be right back." Stephen lifted her leg and placed it on the bench.

"Oh, let me have the notes about the shoe. We need to make a plan here." Stephen reached into his shirt pocket and handed her the pad.

Drew watched Stephen cross the street against traffic, sat up, adjusted her eyesight to the sun, and looked at the notepad. It was not, of course, a real Jimmy Choo shoe, not in a size 14 DD, and not from Snazoo.

Stephen and the cab arrived at the same time. They climbed in the backseat and Drew placed her foot back up on Stephen's lap. "Ice?" Stephen reached into the white plastic bag and withdrew a large bag of Birds Eye frozen peas and held it up. "Close enough." Drew grimaced as he draped it over her injured foot.

"Okay, here we go. The shoe is a Snazoo, whatever that is, in a size 14 DD. Do we think that changes our working theory about this?"

"Snazoo? Never heard of it. No, I don't think it changes the theory at all." Stephen nodded toward the cab driver. "Why would it? Those guys often send messages in this way with these weird kinds of weapons or in the way they place the body."

"Okay, but this is a high heel, for crying out loud, not a fish wrapped in a newspaper. I think it's a stretch."

"Makes perfect sense to me. I think it's a sign of revulsion. Like you said, no mos in the mob. It certainly sends a message."

"But why kill him at all?"

"Same reason we wanted him. The weak link in the chain. Do you really imagine he would have held up under questioning? I don't." Stephen rolled the window partway down.

"That's right. That guy would have folded like a cheap suit. It was probably pre-emptive. Let's start with the computer stuff, see if anything comes of it. Although I doubt it. Then maybe take a look again at the bar where he worked. Maybe something will come of it, maybe not. But they have to know more about this guy than we do. Remind me to ask them if they found a cell phone. I didn't see one in the apartment. What else are we forgetting?"

"Nothing that I can think of right now. I'm sure there'll be more later. Right now, I'm napping."

"And dreaming about Dr. Dreamy?"

"Yep." Stephen slumped back in the seat careful not to disturb Drew's foot. "Although I don't think I'll get very far with that since I have frozen food sitting on my crotch."

Stephen drifted into a light sleep as Drew watched the rapidly passing series of gas stations and strip malls. The Cape was such a contrast to Washington, D.C. Long stretches of unused land, no buildings more than three stories and, even in the summer, a scarcity of humans. The biggest difference was not in the numbers of people but the kind. Everyone here seemed genuinely more joyful. Not just the summer throngs, either, but the locals, the folks who worked four or five jobs just to be able to afford a small apartment near the water seemed imbued with a buoyant contentment. Washington, by contrast, had the energy of a city on the edge of a nervous breakdown. Rows of beige and gray buildings built in the unfortunate architecture of the 1960s, massive structures as distinct from one another as Monopoly hotel pieces. And streaming between and among them were skittering gaggles of middle-aged bureaucrats in rumpled out-of-season suits. This phenomenon quadrupled at the start of the congressional session.

Maggie referred to it as the curtain of mediocrity descending that din you hear is every good idea and honorable intention crowding onto the last Metroliner out. Maggie said D.C. stood for Dreary Central.

"Which one are you thinking about?" Stephen shifted in his seat, eyes still closed.

"Neither, I'm thinking about the case."

"You're a very bad liar. Maggie is haunting you. I can feel it from here." Stephen gave a crooked smile and opened one eye.

"Ya don't have to get all accurate about it. That helps no one."

"Sorry." Stephen opened the other eye and sat up in his seat. "You're leaking."

"I'm pretty sure I'm not. It wasn't that kind of haunting."

"Okay, that's icky. Leaking water. This bag is leaking water. All over me." Stephen rolled down the window and held the bag out until all the water had been dislodged." Great, now I get to spend the rest of the day looking like I peed my pants. We need to stop at the condo before we go anywhere. This is disgusting, not to mention freezing cold."

Drew was laughing full force as she sat up. "Oh, my gosh, you're soaked. I'm sorry. We'll stop so you can change and… uh…re-inflate? Is that the right word? No wonder those guys in

Alaska can't get wives. And all this time, I thought it was their bathing habits."

"I can't believe you just said that. Is nothing sacred?" Stephen folded his hands over his lap laughing.

"Well, yeah, some things are but certainly not that." The cab pulled over to the side of the road in front of Angel's. "Come on, I'll hobble in front of you so nobody sees. Then we interview the co-workers."

Chapter Eighteen

It was obviously a setup of some kind. The back of Lucky was cavernous in size, snaking back and around in a series of rooms for nearly a block. As the bartender led Drew and Stephen around the last corner, the corridor spilled out into a room the size of a small gymnasium.

Rows and rows of six-foot folding tables were lined up in perfect horizontal lines. At precise one-foot intervals were black plastic placemats with "Dingo" printed in four-inch block letters across the top. Two young bar boys were setting silver folding chairs in front of each mat. In the front of the room was a good-sized stage. Across the back was a billboard-sized poster with the word "Dingo" spelled out in human letters.

The D was a beautiful black drag queen in a silver sequin high-collar dress, posed slightly bent over with her arms supplying the curve of the D. Underneath the D in descending small letters was spelled out Donita Facelift. The next was a big blond Gloria Gaynor look-alike dressed in an A-line deep blue velvet knee-length dress and a lot of large oversized costume jewelry. His body was arranged laboriously to form an I. Behind him read Ida Slapter. The N was a quite young-looking Hispanic man dressed in a sea green chiffon gown and elbow-length white gloves. He bent in the three-quarters pose necessary to form the N. It read Nidda Biggerone. The G, which actually looked a bit more like a C, was a middle-aged Asian drag queen in a bright yellow plastic mini-skirt and white go-go boots. Her name was Ginger Vitus. The O was a large, very heavy, and indeed mustached bear-like man dressed in a red and white gingham-checked jumper with a slightly stained white blouse. He sported two red bows in tiny pigtails. Her name read Olive Inatrailer. In the middle of the stage was a series of risers painted in black squares with white borders. They were aligned in neat rows underneath the lettered drag queens.

"What is this, the drag queen U.N. or something?" Drew continued to scan the room.

"We're setting up now," the bartender said.

"I can see. Setting up for what exactly?"

"Almost tea dance. Gets jammed. In another hour, it will be buttplug to belt buckle in here. Not a seat to be had. I'll get Kenneth, the owner, he's backstage."

"Stephen, are you getting this at all?" Drew pulled one of the silver chairs away from the table and sat down.

"Not really. I've been in this bar lots of times in the past when it was still Cape Cod Piece, but I never even knew this was back here till now. Whatever it is, it's quite a setup, I'll say that." The bartender returned alone.

"Kenneth is making some adjustments backstage with the lighting, he'll be right out. Can I go now? I need to start setting up the front bar."

"You told him we were from Washington, right?" Stephen said, slightly more loudly than he had intended.

"Yes, and he was very impressed by that. So when he's done setting up the lighting, like I said, he'll be out. That it?"

"Yeah, that's it. But don't leave town." Stephen stared at the bartender.

"Okay, how about if I just leave the room?" The bartender disappeared down the long corridor they had come through.

"Why did you do that?"

"Do what?"

"That. That 'I'm a boy, watch me piss over the Volkswagen thing' you always do. We might want to interview that guy, ya know."

"Yeah, okay. I didn't like his attitude."

"As long as you had a good reason."

"Hey, why with all these pictures of these drag performers is there no picture of Mango in here? I thought he was kind of a big deal. Like a headliner or something."

"Oh, they had to take that down. Poor thing. I really liked him. He was sweet, sort of like a lost boy type." The voice whizzed by both of them, then back. "I can't believe he's gone. Life, as they say, is too weird." He whizzed back and forth a few more times.

"Could you stop for a minute?" Drew said. The figure stopped in front of her. He was wearing pancake makeup the color of white icing. On his head sat a white eighteenth century-style wig. He held a white feather fan in his left hand. The top half of him was dressed in a T-shirt that read, "Get Lucky." His bottom half was a round tabletop draped in a floor-length white linen table cloth; it had a Plexiglas top with a two-inch rim around it. Although they were not visible, he was clearly wearing Rollerblades. "Don't tell me, let me guess," Drew said.

"The Ghost of Appetizer Tables Past," Stephen offered.

"Close. It's hard to tell without the dress on. Marie Antoinette. My partner, Anna, and I are the 'Let Them Eat Cake' tables. Actually, it's 'Let Them Eat Granola Bars' now. Atkins was killing our business. Of course, if these guys knew how much trans fat was in those granola bars, they wouldn't eat them, either."

"Okay, Marie, I'm Drew and this is Stephen. We'd like to talk to you for a few minutes. Sounds like you knew Alex Rodriguez pretty well. Is that right?"

"Actually, my given name is William. My drag name is Iatta Cupcake. Don't know anybody named Alex. Anyway, gotta practice. Got in big trouble last tea dance for running into some big guy with the front of the table. Actually, he ran into me, but you know how it is, the table always gets the blame." With that, he whizzed back and forth a few more times, then stopped. "Gets a little tight in this middle aisle with both me and Anna rollin' up and down here."

"Who's Anna again?" Stephen reached out and lightly grabbed the Plexiglas rim of the table.

"My partner, Anna Rexia. She's the other table. She's a little bigger than me because she used to sell other things besides food, like cigarettes and porn and lube and shit. But now it's all bottled water and granola bars. Whatever happened to the eighties, huh?" With that, table number two came spinning around the corner.

"Sorry I'm late, doll. Couldn't get that shuttle boat to come to Long Point to save my life today. Oh, company. Hello there." Anna Rexia whizzed by at a high rate of speed.

They made several more passes up and down the aisle, nearly missing each other. "Iatta, if you don't learn to take the corners better, you're gonna get creamed."

"You're too big, Anna, you keep getting in my way. We need to cut that thing down," Iatta said, stopping in front of Anna.

"I know, ironic isn't it? Don't touch my table, Cupcake. How many times I gotta tell ya, don't touch my table." Iatta and Anna stood eye to eye for a brief moment. "Okay, come on, we gotta dress." Before Drew or Stephen could stop them, they flew around the corner.

"Now I really have seen everything. I'm getting tired of waiting for this Kenneth guy, I'll tell ya that." Drew started hobbling around the room.

"I'll go get him." Stephen headed for the backstage area. As he reached the turn by the stage, a blindingly bright series of stage lights came on. The double doors to the corridor opened and a rush of young men began scrambling for seats at the tables. In only a few minutes, the entire room was filled with the smell of suntan lotion, salt, sweat, and lemon vodka.

Iatta Cupcake peered around the corner of the stage and began waving her fan furiously in the air. Once she had caught the attention of Stephen and Drew, she mouthed the words "move back." Stephen and Drew moved to stand against the back wall. A moment later, Iatta and Anna Rexia came screaming around the corner and whizzed up and down the center aisle several times. The customers began hooting and hollering and waving money in the air. Anna and Iatta passed out square white cards and what appeared to be sets of glitter-covered quarters in plastic baggies. Money was changing hands at a rapid rate.

"Five dollars a card, boys, six for twenty five," Anna and Iatta were shouting to the crowd. "Two minutes to go time." The last few exchanges took place, and Anna and Iatta raced up the center aisle, blew a kiss to the crowd, and were temporarily gone.

The lights dimmed, then a follow-spot spilled a circle of yellow-white light stage left. A loud low male voice from offstage boomed, "Ladies and gentlemen and those still undecided, please help me welcome the Queens of Dingo...Miss Donita Facelift, Miss Ida Slapter, Miss Nidda Biggerone, Miss Ginger Vitus, and last but not least Miss Olive Inatrailer." As each name was called, each star took her place underneath her picture on the top step of the riser.

"And now those beautiful boys of summer, the Lucky Charms." With that, a flock of shirtless well-muscled tan young men wearing only a variety of brightly colored Speedos walked out and formed a line across the front of the stage and began posing in various positions. All the stage lights dimmed. The Lucky Charms turned in sync to face stage left.

"And now filling in today by popular demand, please help me welcome the one, the only, Lois Carmen Denominator." She was dressed in a silver sequin low-cut blouse in a country style, her wig was clearly of the Southern "the higher the hair, the closer to god" style, and her skirt was composed of a variety of brightly colored crinolines, so many that the portion around her waist stuck out so straight you could have played cards on it. As she twirled across the stage, she resembled an Andy Warhol version of a car wash. She stopped just to the left of the Dingo riser. "Okay, boys, bring me my balls."

She swept her arm out toward the Lucky Charms. From stage right, four Lucky Charms appeared, pushing a large steel cage filled with volleyballs, each with a letter and number. "On your mark, get ready, get set, let's play dingo!" The four Lucky Charms turned the cage several times until one volleyball dropped out of the hole in the bottom. One of the Charms took the ball over to Lois and held it aloft. "I 16, that's Ida Slapter 16." She threw the volleyball to the nearest Charm, who, in turn, threw it to the first Charm lined up at the front of the stage. That Charm climbed the long set of risers until he reached the second to the top tier. He turned and stood just below Ida and held the volleyball at chest height.

"Ida never slapped her if she was as cute as that boy. Okay, next." The next number was O 24. The routine was repeated in a long series until someone near the front of the room yelled, "Dingo," and threw his arms in the air. Anna Rexia and Iatta Cupcake, who had resumed their positions in the center aisle busily selling bottled water and small snacks to the throng, zoomed, one in back of the other, toward the winner. They each handed him a silver and black envelope, and the game resumed.

Drew was laughing. "This is too funny. This is why it's good to be gay. No one else could think up this shit."

"I can't believe I didn't know about this. Well, that, at least, explains all those bingo games in his apartment. So at least we got something out of this trip," Stephen said.

"What do you mean? How?"

"It's a bingo game. A live version. Brilliant really. I wonder how much ecstasy went into this little invention."

"Really? Oh. Oh. I see. Bingo. Dingo. Drag queen bingo. Too funny. Well, we aren't making much progress here. I think we better come back when this is over. Let's see if the cops have made any progress on the computer stuff. I think we best invite these girls down to the station if we want to get serious interviews out of them, don't you?"

"Yep. Let's go see what the hard drive holds."

Chapter Nineteen

"A more thorough examination." Drew was beginning to like the way the words tasted in her mouth. As she tumbled the words around, she continued trying to insert it. But no matter what angle she tried, from the left, from the right, or dead on, it simply would not fit. Her frustration building, she leaned back in the chair, sighed, grasped it with both hands, and pushed as hard as she could. She came close to sliding completely out of the chair.

"What in the world are you doing over there?" Stephen stared at her blankly.

"Isn't it obvious?" Drew slumped forward in the chair and put her head down on the desk.

"Not entirely, no."

"It won't fit. I think it's just too big."

"Too big? They come in different sizes? That can't be right. I don't know why you're freaking out, you've only done this like a million times."

"I'm telling you, no matter how I try it, I can't get it in there."

"Oh, for crying out loud, here, I'll do it." Stephen turned the computer disk over and slid it into the A drive. "There, you had it backward. Now see what's on there. The one I just finished had nothing on it but a bunch of Mapquest directions to places in New York. Total garbage. There are like forty more of these."

"Hey, thanks. I must be over tired. Mapquest maps of where

in New York?"

"Don't know yet. I'm running cross-checks on the addresses. My guess is gay bars. But who knows? We could use some more help on this. Any idea when that might happen?" Stephen rolled his chair up next to hers and started punching the computer keys, opening the A drive, and scanning the index.

"No, I think those Boston guys have lost interest in this. Last call, they said they might not make it down here until the weekend. It's all terrorism now. Organized Crime has a whole new meaning. Plus which, according to them, there's only like two guys left in the mob up there. The rest are all either too old or young and stupid enough to get caught without informants. Looks like it's just us. They're faxing some stuff down. People they think are 'possibles' because of the way it went down or their connection to the 'family.' But at least they're still interviewing the Baychamp boys. I guess their high-priced mob lawyer abandoned them. Maybe something will come of that."

"Great. Nothing like backup. How are we supposed to decide who killed this guy? I don't know anything about the mob. And something tells me we aren't going to find it in this guy's computer. This disk is all this bingo shit. Nothing. Unless a bingo stalker killed him, this is nothing. Speaking of....when are we interviewing those guys back at the bar?"

"They agreed to come over here right after they're done." Drew looked at her watch. "Which should be in about half an hour, by my count. I asked for all the Dingos, the hostess, and the tables. And if you're going to say it, get it out of your system now, so it doesn't leak out during the interviews. Nothing on this disk, either."

"Say what?" Stephen popped the next disk into the computer.

"I'm serious. It'll be hard enough to get through these interviews. We're interviewing tables, for god's sake. That's enough weirdness for one afternoon. Just say it already. You know you're dying to." Drew continued flipping open the documents on the computer.

Stephen leapt up out of his chair. "The dingo ate my baby!

The dingo ate my baby!" He sat back down.

"Feel better now?"

"God, yes. I've been holding that in for two hours. You know, isn't it interesting that whatever the circumstances, there's always some Meryl Streep quote that's just exactly right?"

"Yes, she has quite a range. Hey, there are actually some interesting things on this one. Some notes and some letters. Look." Drew turned the computer screen toward Stephen.

He began scrolling through the documents. There were some random notes about the dingo show, some names, and phone numbers. The next five or six pages contained what appeared to be an actual written set of instructions to the dingo game. They contained all the names and descriptions of the drag performers, the Lucky Charms, even the Let Them Eat Cake tables right down to the powdered wigs. The instructions appeared to be typed on some kind of form. "This is sort of weird. What is this form? Why all this detail?"

"Is there a date on it? That might help."

"I don't see one." Stephen continued to scroll down the pages. No, no date on the document itself, but it was last saved on this disk as an updated version about a month ago. So I guess he was working on this recently. Let's print it. Maybe there will be a form number on here."

"Well, that may be interesting, but unless this guy was killed by a bingo purist, all this dingo stuff seems irrelevant to me." Drew walked over and grabbed the documents off the printer. "Yep, it's a form of some kind. A federal form at that. Not one I know, though. You ever seen this before?" Drew handed the papers to Stephen.

"Nope. Let me call Spree, I'll have her run it down. It may be nothing, but it's the only thing of substance we've found, if it is of substance."

"There's a couple of guys out here to see you." The young officer was pointing down the long hall toward the front of the police station. "Should I bring them in or are you getting them?"

"Thanks, officer. Yes, you can bring them in here if you would please. We don't want to take up more of your space than absolutely necessary. Thanks for being so accommodating, we really appreciate it."

"No problem." The officer disappeared down the darkly paneled hallway.

"Stephen, you should take the lead with these guys. They might respond better to you. It should be a friendly undertaking anyway since we just want to know whatever they knew about him."

The officer escorted in two late-thirty-something men dressed in T-shirts and shorts. They could have been tourists from Anywhere, USA, except for the ghost-white makeup and the thick black painted eyebrows arched in a state of constant surprise. Stephen smiled and made the introductions. They all took seats around the only table in the room.

"Iatta, the little table. Seeing as that's how we met. My real name is William Brill."

"And I'm Gregory Bradley. Sorry for the makeup. We don't want you to think we didn't take this seriously, but this stuff is a bitch to get off and we have three more shows to do today. So, sorry. Hope that's okay." Gregory extended his hand.

"I understand. That's fine. Can you tell me how long you've been doing this? Did Alex Rodriguez work there the whole time? That's Mango, in case you don't know." Stephen tapped his pen lightly on the legal pad sitting in front of him.

"We've been there like eight years. Or will be at the end of the season. We started together. Used to do the same gig in New York for a big caterer. Still do in the winter. Got a steady gig of parties for them at Rockefeller Center," William said.

"You know the straight crowd loves it. I prefer ice skating anyway. It's really my first love. You know all those kids who get up at five a.m. to practice skating all through their lives? Here's two that didn't make it to the Olympic Games." Gregory pointed to himself, then to William.

"Oh, so you grew up together?" Stephen scribbled some notes on the pad.

"Oh, god no. Different coasts. I'm west, he's east." William pointed to himself first. "We answered the same ad when we were in New York trying not to starve to death. Not a big secondary market for failed ice skaters. The odds were pretty high we would meet eventually. He's a little older, so we did the skating circuit at different times when we were young."

"I'm like six months older, thank you. Anyway, we've worked together a long time. And that's it. We just work together. Nothing else," Gregory said.

"As if I would," William said.

"As if I'd ask," Gregory said.

"Okay. How did you get the job at Lucky? Isn't that the old Cape Cod Piece? Or am I wrong about that?" Stephen asked William.

"Oh, yeah, but not for years now. Leather bars went way out here for a few years. It's been a few things since then. Lucky is just its latest incarnation. We've done the show a few places, too. This is just the biggest place here. As you saw, it's huge. They moved it because they needed more space," William said.

"Actually, I got us the jobs there. It was at a different bar then. I think it was called Midnight," Gregory said.

"Yes. Midnight. He called me in New York and said he thought we could get a gig out here over the summer. The season was much shorter then, just three months, really. Now it runs almost till November. But anyway, that's how we got the jobs," William said.

"The bar owner hired us. He was starting this show and needed at least two guys who could skate. The money was really good, even back then. And the catering falls off a lot in summer because all the money people are in the Hamptons. It worked out great for us. We spend almost all year out here now," Gregory said.

"So Kenneth hired you?" Stephen asked.

"No. That's the guy that owns Lucky. This was Brian Chester. He owns the Boat Dock. Has forever. The show moved to Lucky about three years ago now. We all just went with it. The whole group," Gregory said.

"What a cluster that was. Remember?" William said to Gregory.

"What's that mean? You mean cluster as in you all moved in

135

a cluster?" Drew said.

"No, he means cluster, as in, you should excuse the expression, cluster fuck. Trouble. Big trouble. Mango and Brian really got into it over that. I thought the whole thing was going to fall apart. They still hate each other's guts, I think. Don't you think so, Cupcake?"

"Totally."

"So you both have known Mango a long time then? What can you tell us about him?" Stephen said.

"We worked together for a long time, but we, or at least I, didn't know him well at all. He didn't spend a lot of time with the great unwashed. He's the star." Gregory held his hands up in Hollywood fashion. "Or was, I guess. How weird and gruesome. Did he really get killed with a high heel? Anyway, the only thing that guy ever wanted to know from me was how much cash we brought in."

"Know anything about his friends, who he hung out with? Do you know if he used drugs? "Anything?" Drew said. "Anything at all? Even maybe who else we could talk to?"

"Drugs? Yep. Could definitely be. He was quite the party boy. The busiest bottom in this town. I don't play with drugs myself but could be for him. What do you think?" Gregory said to William.

"Beats me. I don't pay that much attention to that stuff. It's hard enough for me just to get through my own day. But I've seen him out at the clubs a lot. So could be. I don't think he had many friends, though. He spent a lot of time on the show. He was always in Lucky. Little bit of a control freak if you know what I mean. But with all that money at stake, I guess that's why he was so successful." William rubbed his fingers together as if he were counting money.

"You've said that like two or three times now. About the money. How much money are we talking about?" Stephen said.

"I don't know what the whole show brings in, but our part alone is almost six figures each," William said.

"That's a lot of bottled water. You guys selling anything else in there?" Drew asked.

"No. The snacks are a small part of it. Most of it is the game itself. Five bucks a card. Most of those guys play three or four a game, some as many as ten. Three shows a day, four in high season. Hundred guys at a time, plus drinks. He was making out big-time," William said.

"Enough to support a drug habit," Drew said to Stephen.

"Enough to support ten," William said.

There was a knock on the door. "Hey, there's one more guy out here now. Should I bring him back or wait?" The officer half-smiled.

"Yeah, now's fine, thanks." Drew got up and extended her hand to the two men. "Thanks very much for coming. And if we could just ask you to not discuss what we talked about here, that would be really helpful."

"Well, that doesn't make much sense," Drew said after Gregory and William left.

"I know. Why go to the mob for money if you're rolling it? Although his apartment sure didn't seem like he was rolling in it. Even that computer of his was at least five years old. But if those guys are making that much, they must be right about the money."

"Maybe the mob had something else on him. Maybe it was blackmail."

"Something more than being a drag queen who presides over a live bingo game with half-naked men. What would that be exactly? What else is there?" Stephen grabbed a white mug from the corner table and filled it with coffee. "Can we take a break after this next guy? This coffee tastes like shit. I need the real stuff."

"Yeah, sure."

"Who's next anyway? Do we know?" Stephen thought better of it and set the coffee cup down next to the pot.

There was a loud whooshing sound, and they looked toward the door. Lois Carmen Denominator's crinolines were still vibrating as she approached the table. "Sorry, but no time to change. It takes like an hour to get in and out of these. Oh, coffee, good." Lois made her way to the coffee station, sending three chairs scattering in the process. "So what do you want to know about her?" Lois turned to face them.

"Everything you know. Anything, friends, acquaintances, boyfriends. How long did you know...did you say her?" Stephen stood up.

"She preferred that. This is just work for me, all this mess. Brought me a good livin', too. Better than being a retail queen, that's for sure. But it was real life for her."

"You sound like you knew her better than you said you did. That's a lot of empathy for someone you hardly know." Stephen sat back down in his chair and started writing.

"Is it?"

"Seems so, yes. So you knew her pretty well then. What about how she spent her time away from work? Did you know her socially? Her friends? Did she have a boyfriend? Girlfriend?" Stephen continued writing. Lois refilled her coffee cup for the third time. They both turned toward a sudden soft buzzing sound.

"Sorry. Cell. You two continue. I'll take this in the hall." Drew flipped the phone open on her way out.

"Did you know her friends? How she spent her time?"

"Not really. We weren't friends. I'm not sure she really had that many. She was the workingest girl I ever saw. I'll say that for her. Plus, she was kind of a sad mac type. A loner. I think she just put everything she had into the show. I know lots of performers like that. You know, all razzle dazzle on stage, then fizzle off stage. This one, she left it all on stage."

"Stephen, we need to talk. Can you come out here for a second?" Drew was standing in the doorway holding the cell phone to her shoulder.

"Uh, sure, excuse me just a minute." Stephen closed the door behind him. "What's up?"

"It's Dr. Falon. He found something. He thinks we need to go back over there."

"Found what?" Stephen whispered.

"I don't know exactly. Something about a piece of paper. How much longer with this guy? Is it going anywhere? I need to tell Dr. Falon something here."

"I think this is over. If not, we can come back to it. Doesn't seem to be any connecting the dots from here to anything remotely mob-like. I must get coffee, but we could get back over there within the hour."

"That's what I'll tell him. And take those disks, we'll look at them on the way over on the laptop. It will save us some time."

Chapter Twenty

"This is the long road to nowhere." Drew flipped up the laptop screen.

"Lady, this is the most direct route." The cab driver glared at her in the rearview.

Drew looked back, confused. "Oh, no, I was talking to him." Drew pointed to Stephen. "Not you. Sorry for the confusion."

"You're the only person I know who can be in conflict with someone and not even know it," Stephen whispered. "Which is the road to nowhere? The interviews or the documents?"

"Yes." Drew was squinting into the screen. "You think I'm wrong?"

"Never. I don't see how these performers are ever going to lead us to some mob connection. They seem like they hardly knew the guy. I know we've only talked to a few of them, but there doesn't seem to be even a thread of a social connection among this crowd. They don't even think he had drug issues. That seemed obvious to me, and I only met the guy for like half an hour."

"Maybe the stuff from Boston will be there when we get back. These disks are worthless. It's like everything you never wanted to know about bingo. When did Spree think she might have something on that form?" Drew closed the cover of the laptop.

"Not long, she was calling OMB. They're starting to ask questions back there. She's covering as best she can, but we're going to get phone calls soon. So what did the coroner say exactly?

Why the rush?"

"Said he found something he thought we would want to see right away. Something he found in the body. Doesn't that sound like a pleasant way to spend an afternoon?"

"In the body? Like inside the body?"

"Yeah. And yes, it's weird and no, I can't imagine what it is and yes, I hope it's an inanimate object and not something we didn't know was in the human body until the coroner yanks it out. That about cover it for ya?"

"Pretty much. Hold your nose, here we go." Stephen held the door out for her and helped her out of the cab.

Dr. Falon led Drew and Stephen to the same small space in the back they had been in earlier. There was a large microscope set up in the middle of the desk.

"I feel a bit foolish about this. But I didn't find it in the first go-round. It wasn't until you asked me to re-examine the wounds for consistency with a professional killing as it were. I started digging around a bit, not to be gruesome about it, mind you, respect for the dead and all that. But it was so deep in the body cavity, I think I'd have missed it altogether if I hadn't had that second look."

"What is it exactly?" Drew stood shoulder to shoulder with Falon over the microscope.

"It appears to be a piece of paper, could be cloth, it held up unusually well for paper if it is paper, with some writing on it."

"Writing? What kind of writing? Like a note? Like a suicide note?" Stephen said.

"No, a most unlikely suicide, I would think. It's not all that clear. Seems to be some numbers. Perhaps a receipt of some kind. I was hoping you might know. Have a look."

Drew closed one eye and looked in the lens. With some adjustment of the eye piece, she eventually was able to make out a series of smudged squiggles. "I can't really make this out. Is there any way to enhance this to make it clearer?"

"I've been trying, but not so far. My scope is not that big. And the paper, well, let's just say various fluids are on it."

"Can you take it out of there for a second? Stephen, hand me your phone. Where did you find this again? I mean where in the body exactly?" Drew lined the phone up with the paper as close as she could get it and snapped six digital pictures.

"In the primary wound site. Where you would have seen the heel sticking in. Right here." Falon poked himself in the throat at the exact spot. "It was in pretty deep, like maybe it had been on the bottom of the shoe's heel or something like that."

"Okay, you need to hold onto this for now. If I get nothing off these pictures, which is doubtful, we'll have to ship this off to the lab. But for now, can you just hold onto it?"

"Sure."

"Thanks, Dr. Falon. I'll be back in touch within the hour. By the way, drug screen?"

"Negative for everything. No puncture wounds indicating needles, either."

"Okay."

"This case gets weirder by the minute." Drew was shifting in her seat.

"Tell me about it. You don't really think this phone picture is going to get it, do you?"

"Not really, but it's all I could think of. It's not like we have lab guys up here. Nothing else in this case has worked out the way I thought it would, so maybe just this one time, we'll get lucky."

"Yes, lucky. That totally defines us. But just in case, what is plan B?"

"I have no idea."

"So the same as before then?"

"Yeah, pretty much."

They rode in a fidgety silence until they reached the police station back in Provincetown.

"Give me your phone and cross your fingers. And hand me that cord so I can hook this up."

"So if you don't know anything about computers, how is it exactly that you know how to do this?" Stephen handed Drew the phone and the cord in one motion.

"Gee, I wonder. Let's see...pictures, uploading...any of that registering with you yet?"

"Oh, yes. Sorry. I didn't know Maggie would take pictures that way. She was such a..."

"Control freak?"

"I was going to say perfectionist. But I defer. That working yet?"

"It takes a minute. Okay, I'll stop saying evil things about Maggie, so you don't have to spend all your time defending her. Here we go. Hey, it worked. Sort of." Drew rolled her chair up close to the computer screen. "Wow. That's way better than I thought it would be. Of course, you still can't tell what it is. At least I can't. You?"

"Not a clue." They stared at the screen for several minutes. "It's just so smudged. Looks like just random circles, are they circles? And lines. Looks like a big old sack of nothing to me. Maybe Xs and Os. It looks like the same thing over and over again."

"A tic-tac-toe game? No. That's too weird even for this case. Some numbers maybe that got smeared? Let's enlarge it a little." What filled the screen were larger versions of what they had just seen. "Well, that was helpful. Really big squiggles."

"Try reducing it instead," Stephen said.

"Oh, that's better. How did you know that?"

"I didn't. I still think it's a pattern. It repeats see, these are all the same and these are all the same. See."

"Not really, but okay. Write this down then and let's see what we think of it. In the meantime, I'm calling Falon. This definitely needs to go to the lab." Drew took out her cell phone and punched in the numbers.

Stephen wrote down what he saw on the screen. "Okay, this is the best I can do." He handed the paper to Drew. It read: 01000 100010010010100111001000111101001111.

Chapter Twenty-one

"Did a leprechaun throw up in here?" Stephen waited for his eyes to adjust to the light.

"I thought you would like this place. It's the only Irish restaurant in town. I'll give you that it's a little overdecorated." Drew flagged the hostess, who was awash in bright green from head to toe, her crayon green Nikes glowed with bargain bin confidence.

"A little overdecorated? I would say so. This is how I know for sure that you're only half Irish." Stephen slid into the green plastic booth. "You think the food in an Irish restaurant is actually going to be good." Stephen flipped open the shamrock-shaped menu.

"I don't think one bowl of stew will bring your life to a screeching halt or anything. Now, what about this number?"

"Stew please." Stephen folded his menu and handed it back to the waitress. "I don't know. Here, let's see." He took out a black flair pen and wrote the number on the white paper tablecloth between them. "Clearly, it's too long to be a combination to a safe or a locker, right?"

"Right. What has that many numbers in it? Let's see, how many numbers is this anyway? The repetition is blinding." Drew counted the numbers with her finger. "Forty. What has forty numbers in it? A bank account number? It looks like those numbers on the bottom of my checks. You know what I mean?"

"I do. But aren't those numbers all different? It's the repetition that makes it so strange. Maybe that in itself means something. Stephen ran his fingers over the number. "There's eighteen ones and twenty-two zeros."

"What about something like eighteen and twenty-two or just 1,822. Does that mean anything?" Drew wrote the numbers on the tablecloth.

Stephen blew large breaths onto the stew in an effort to cool it. "I'm glad we did that because that means nothing as far as I can tell. How's the corned beef and cabbage there, Bridget?"

"Repulsive. You get to be right again. That's two for two for you today. Mark the moment. You could cover Jennifer Beals in cabbage, and I still don't think I could bear it."

"Get real. She is totally hot."

"I know, you gotta love those *L Word* women. And how about that prison scene? How come in all the million bazillion ACT UP demonstrations we got arrested at, we never got to have hot sex in prison?"

"Speak for yourself." Stephen smiled.

"How come you never told me that?"

"Because I didn't want you to stage a nutty on me because you didn't think I wasn't taking it seriously. No one could be serious enough for you in those days." Stephen swiftly looked down as if he were expecting an incoming airstrike.

"Yeah, I know. I can't talk about that now. So this number means nothing to me. You?"

"Yes, this means nothing to me, either. What else?"

"Too long for a phone number, not enough variety for a bank account number, not an address or a ZIP code, not a license number, not a—"

"Wait a minute, what was the number on that form we found in his computer? What about that?"

"No. Good idea, though. But that was a much shorter number and it had letter in it. You know, OMB numbers. I'll check when we get back, but I'm sure I'm right, Bridget." Stephen smiled and wiped the gravy from his chin.

"Funny. So we're back to square one on this. Maybe the

Boston office will have some ideas. Hey, maybe it's their file number on the Gambini case." Drew handed her still full plate back to the waitress who looked disappointed, but not even a little surprised. "Do you have any cake?"

"Yes, we have strawberry shortcake, apple brown betty cake, which is more apple and brown than cake really, and one chocolate with vanilla icing." The waitress shifted her hand to her hip with slight impatience, certain the inedible corned beef and cabbage meant she had already forfeited her tip.

"I'll have the chocolate. And some decaf coffee with some milk if you don't mind. So we have nothing." Drew stared at the tablecloth.

"Not nothing. We have the shoe, after all, and the lab still has to weigh in on this number. Plus we don't have any of the mob stuff from Boston yet. So we have a lot more than nothing. I can't believe you're having cake." Stephen leaned back in his seat as the waitress set the enormous three-layer chocolate cake down in front of Drew.

"I have to eat something, and at least I know I'll like the cake. Here, there's enough here to feed Killarney, have some. Oh, it actually is really good." Drew licked a small bit of icing from her lower lip. "I'm getting tired. My brain is like on triple overtime. Aren't you?"

"I don't usually eat sugar, but I'll make an exception in this case. Hey, this is good. Tastes homemade. Maybe they should make this place a bakery instead. Might be more profitable." Stephen licked the white icing from the prongs of his fork. "Hey, wait a minute." Stephen spoke with the fork still in his mouth.

"What? Did you poke yourself with that fork? You don't need to fellate it, you know. And don't you dare get blood on my cake. I've had enough bodily fluids for one day." Stephen sat with the fork in his mouth. "Hey, did you really hurt yourself? Stephen?"

"I think I know what that is." Stephen took the fork out of his mouth and began pointing it at the number on the table. "It's binary. Drew, that's it! It's a binary number. How could I not have known that?"

"What do you mean? Binary, is that like foreign or something?

Like Italian? Something the mob would use?"

Stephen was laughing. "No, it's not Italian, goofball. Binary. How did you get through Catholic school and not know what a binary number is? Binary, Drew, binary." Stephen continued to point the fork, now with increasing force.

"I know this is hard for you to believe, but you just repeating the word binary like a savant, doesn't really help me understand what it means. And put that fork down before you hurt one of us."

"It's a way of coding numbers in ones and zeros. It's what they use to write computer code, things like that. Understand?" Stephen fidgeted with the fork in his hands.

"No, I don't understand. What do you mean code numbers? It's a code? What kind of code?"

"No, not a secret code code. A way of coding." Stephen held up his hands as if they contained all the answers.

"Again with the repeating and not helping."

"Okay, here, like when you go into the grocery store and there is a bar code on the cereal box."

"Right."

"Well, it's always coded in ones and zeros. It's how they do the pricing. That way, the computer can read it. Get it?"

"Oh. I never knew that. Not exactly, no. But whatever. Do you know how to uncode it?"

"Decode it."

"Whatever. You really milk these moments, don't you? Where you know something that I don't. It's really unattractive. Anyway, can you decode it, oh, genius one?" Drew bowed toward Stephen with an exaggerated flourish.

"Actually, I haven't done that in a long time, and this is a pretty long one. Let's go online and see if we can find a converter." Stephen reached under the table and withdrew his laptop.

"How are you going to dial up from here? It's not like we have a phone." Drew cleared some space on the table.

"It's wireless. The whole world is wireless now. With the exception of you, of course." Stephen turned on the computer and brought up the Google Web site.

"No need to get snotty about it. So how do you do this?"

"Wait. Let me find a site." Stephen typed "binary conversion table" in the search area and pressed the button. "Oh, good, look there's like fifty of them. God bless Google."

"When exactly have you done this before? Are you some secret nerd or something?"

"I used to have to do it every year. The Marys taught me."

"The Marys? As in *the* Marys? As in your Aunts Mary?"

"Now who's the savant? And I think it's Aunt Marys. Yes, they used to do all of our birthday cakes that way. Instead of say ten candles on the cake or one big number ten candle, they would spell out our ages on the top of the cake in the binary equivalent with peppermint sticks and lifesavers. Then all four of them would stand around and wait for us to figure it out."

"So what you're telling me is that your eighty-year-old aunts know binary numbers and I don't."

"Actually, that story had remarkably little to do with you, but, okay, yes. Of course, they weren't eighty then, they were young women. Really smart young women, as a matter of fact. Mary Katherine and Mary Elizabeth were scientists. I think that's how they knew about the binary system. Either that, or it had something to do with the Latin Mass, I'm not sure. Okay, here we go. Here, look." Stephen typed the number and clicked the convert button. He turned the laptop screen toward Drew. The number 6873787179 materialized on the screen. "Wow. How about that. It worked."

"Okay, six, eight, seven, three, seven, eight, seven, one, seven, nine. What does it mean?"

"That would be the second problem. Your turn. I got us this far."

Chapter Twenty-two

The characters resembled those you might find in the discarded pages from the first draft of an Elmore Leonard novel. Bennie "the Boots" Bonato, known for his facility with a shiv he kept hidden in a secret pocket of his trademark black alligator ankle-high boots.

"How can it be a secret if everybody, including the FBI, knows it's there?" Stephen wrote the name on the board.

"Now this is a good question. Okay, here's the next one, Lennie "Fat Boy" Muzuto, a lovely gentleman known for his ability to break a bone so clean and evenly, it almost appears surgical."

"Come on. You must be kidding me." Stephen wrote the name on the board.

"That's what it says." Drew looked down at the file in her lap.

"Not that. I mean rhyming mob guys? Bennie and Lennie. Come on. Tell me the next one's Hennie, right?"

"Oh, I didn't even notice that. Well, they're Italian, that's bound to happen, there are just so many vowels to go around. The next one is Tony 'the Spreader' Bucelli."

"The Spreader? I don't want to know."

"Let's just say it has something to do with a wood chipper and leave it at that. Next is Robert Edward Grambuso."

"No nickname?" Stephen wrote the name on the board.

"No. Wait a minute. Oh, no wonder, he's their accountant.

Well, that's useful. What kind of bullshit list of suspects is this anyway? I think those Boston guys just sent us a bunch of whatever was laying around. I don't think they put one bit of thought into which of these guys might actually be the one." Drew continued flipping through the files on her lap.

"These are like three hundred-pound hardcore mob guys. Don't we think they would have stuck out here just a wee bit? Wouldn't they have sent somebody who would blend in more? Are any of them younger than sixty, for god's sake?" Stephen took one of the files and started flipping through it.

"Doesn't look like it. These guys are all old school mob looks like to me. Unfortunately, it's all we have. And none of them is named Bobbie 'Binary Number' Bullato. Too bad for us. That's starting not to fit so well. None of these guys seems clever or smart enough to leave behind a signature like that. Let's switch gears and do witnesses then." Drew grabbed her legal pad out of her briefcase. "Okay, Iatta Cupcake aka 'the little table.'"

"That's drag queen, not mob guy, right?" Stephen wrote the name in a separate column.

Drew was laughing. "Yes, it does get confusing, though, doesn't it? Okay, Anna Rexia aka 'the big table.' Lois Carmen Denominator aka 'the Emcee.'"

"Lois Carmen." Stephen was writing. "Oh, wait, I'm vibrating." Stephen took the cell phone out of his pocket and flipped it open. He mouthed the word "Spree," walked over, and started scribbling furiously on a legal pad while repeating "uh-huh, yes, and what" in an alternating and increasingly urgent pattern. He clicked the phone closed and stared at Drew.

"What does that face mean? What did she say? Was that about the form or the number? Did she hear from the FBI lab already? Speak."

"Three things, all major major. First, seems old Baychamp Senior flipped on Junior in a hot minute."

"Oh, my god."

"Yep. As soon as the lawyer disappeared, he rolled right over."

"Wow. I guess he figured the lawyer withdrawing was the

mob's sign to him that he was next up on the hit list. They don't leave witnesses behind."

"Probably, plus Senior was none too happy that Junior shot the dog. Apparently, he was really crazy about that dog."

"So? Any news on the Mango connection?"

"Not yet. But they're still questioning them. So far, they're both denying any involvement by Mango. They seem to want to take credit for the whole operation."

"Okay, what else? You said there were three things."

"Right. The next is that the number is right, that means the 6873787179 is right. I still can't believe we were able to do that with a digital picture off a phone. But here is the weird part." Stephen looked down and read from his notes. "The form on Mango's computer, the one with all the dingo directions, that's a trademark application form."

"Get out. You can trademark stuff like that?"

"It's a game, so I guess so. Isn't like Monopoly trademarked? Anyway, that's not the weird part. The weird part is that it's not the only trademark application. There's two. One is this one we have that Mango filled out and the other one was filed by, get this, Brian Chester."

"Yeah, so? Who's Brian Chester? You're looking at me like that should mean something to me."

"Brian Chester is the guy who owns the Boat Dock. Remember those two guys, the tables, were telling us that's where they first did the dingo show years ago."

"I sort of remember that. Anyway, what else did they say?" Drew began reading Stephen's phone notes.

"They said Mango and this Brian Chester guy had a huge falling out when Mango moved the show over to the new bar. They said these two guys hated each other's guts or something to that effect."

"So they both applied to trademark this show. That's interesting, but how in the wide world can this show relate back to the mob in Boston?"

"Maybe it doesn't have anything to do with the mob. If Baychamp Senior is willing to flip on his own son, why wouldn't he give up Mango? In fact, why didn't they try to pin the whole thing on him? So maybe this is the legendary ASRE case." Stephen was writing names and drawing lines between them on the board.

"A Series of Random Events case? You can't be serious. It's mythical, there is no such thing as a real ASRE case. They just tell you that in training so you won't give up on the unsolvable ones. So you'll always be working a new angle. Besides, no way this mob hit comes off without inside help at the bank. And why would Mango take such a low wage job there if he's cashing in on this dingo gig? That makes no sense. A lot of things are worth killing over, but a bingo game? I think you're delusional. You've been cooped up too long. You need to go clear your, well, your head I suppose is the best way to put it."

"What makes you think I haven't had sex?" Stephen said over his shoulder, still writing on the board.

"Oh. Silly me. In that case then, you're just a lunatic."

"I haven't. Yet. But still, I don't like the presumption." Stephen recapped the magic marker and stood back to admire the case map he had drawn on the board.

"I apologize then, for not assuming that you had engaged in random shallow sex with a stranger." Drew stood up and began stuffing the legal pads and computer disks back into her briefcase.

"Apology accepted. Now I say we go see one Mr. Brian Chester. See what we can shake loose." Stephen turned to Drew.

"I will indulge you in this fantasy briefly. But I'm not getting off on some frolic and detour for more than an hour."

"Fantasy and frolic and detour, oh my. After you, Dorothy." Stephen bowed toward the exit.

Chapter Twenty-three

What the Boat Dock lacked in ambiance, essentially a long wooden deck that jutted out over the pale blue water of the bay, it made up for in clientele, scores of well-sculptured young men moving together to the steady thumping beat.

"Only in Provincetown are men this good-looking, as common as grapes." Drew showed her ID to the bouncer at the front entrance.

"Really. Let's peel some." Stephen slid his sunglasses down and peered over the top to get a better look at the crowd. "Let's find Mr. Chester and test my theory. Then I say we have recess."

"He's at the end of the dock at the far bar. Big guy in the red and white shirt." The bartender pointed to the exact opposite end of the dock from where they were standing.

"Stephen, can you go get him? I don't think I can make it all the way down there. I'll wait over at that table on the end. I can't believe there's an empty table out here." Drew moved toward the white plastic table near the end of the small swimming pool on the left side of the deck.

"That's because nobody sits in bars except old people." Stephen smiled.

"Hey, I still have a full head of hair. I win," Drew said, sliding into the chair.

"Ouch. Be right back and I'll bring you a Diet Coke with a witness chaser."

Drew kept her eye on Stephen until he was swallowed by the crowd. The thumping beat of the music was beginning to give her a headache and a foot ache. She propped her foot up on the white plastic chair across from her, leaned back, and closed her eyes.

At least six or seven drops fell before she realized water, or something, was dripping onto her arm. She opened one eye partway and was eye level with a perfectly tanned flat stomach covered with small drops of water and dotted with tiny flecks of damp sand. She looked up.

"Looks like you've strayed a bit off your beaten path." J.J. was standing almost directly over her. Her hair was slick with water, which fell at an increasing rate onto Drew's arm.

"Nice outfit." Drew smiled at the familiar "Contents Under Pressure" T-shirt and the smiley-face Joe Boxer shorts.

"Just in for a bit of a swim. Nice way to end the day. Where's your constant companion, he abandon you for a bit of a nibble or something?" J.J. cocked her head toward the crowd and began drying her hair with an enormous beach towel.

"Actually, he'll be right back. He's getting someone we need to talk to. Can I use that towel for a second? You've made me sort of wet here." Drew grabbed the end of the towel and dried her arm.

"Have I now? An even nicer way to end my day." J.J. ran her fingers through her now half-dry hair and began brushing the sand from her stomach.

"How exactly did you get sand on you from swimming in a pool? And let me see this beach towel." Drew splayed the towel out in front of her. "I think you can tell a lot about a person by what kind of beach towel she chooses."

"Must have been in the towel itself. When you live on the water, you never really get rid of it all. So what's it tell you, then? My towel here."

Drew looked down at the towel. A faded picture of Lucy and Peppermint Patty stared back at her. "I'd say either you've had this since you were seven or you're into American icons in a big way. It also means you're given to a certain ironic sweetness. Close?" Drew looked up at J.J.

"Ironic? Don't think so. Not mine anyway. Was left behind by a passing fancy." J.J. wrapped the towel around her.

"Well, maybe the passing fancy was given to ironic sweetness then."

"Hmm, don't remember really. Didn't stick around long enough to plunge that deep. They rarely do. Well, I best be off. It's bloody freezing out here once you lose the sun. Besides, here comes your boyfriend. How's your foot, then, by the way? Somewhat or no better?"

"Somewhat. Sorry, we really do have to talk to this guy." Drew stood up and suddenly drooped to one side, her bandaged foot now fully asleep.

"Careful there. That doesn't bode well for somewhat better. Perhaps you'll come 'round tomorrow. I'll have another look see. And then maybe dinner? I've still not collected that. I've something I want to show you." J.J. slipped on one beach shoe, then the other.

"Your etchings?" Drew said to J.J.'s back.

"I'm fetching, am I?" J.J. turned to face her.

"No. I mean yes. I said you want to show me your etchings?" Drew smiled.

"Don't know that reference. You'll have to explain it tomorrow night. And catch me up on the big mystery." J.J. winked and scooted toward the exit.

Brian Chester resembled nothing more than an adult version of the slightly overweight, slightly disheveled kid who got picked last for every intramural sports team in high school. Those early scarring events, which turn many toward class clowndom in a desperate effort to find some peer group to glom onto, had instead given him the personality of a steelworker, if the steelworker were a potato. They conducted the interview in his small back office.

"I didn't kill him if that's what you're thinkin'." Brian Chester lit his third cigarette of the last ten minutes. The air was now a light blue haze. "Not that I'm sorry he's dead."

"Why's that, Mr. Chester?" Drew was coughing steadily.

"My mother always told me to say something nice about the dead. He's dead. How nice." Chester sneered into his cigarette.

"Right. But why? Didn't you used to work together?" Stephen handed Drew a perfectly ironed white cotton handkerchief, a remnant of well-learned Catholic manners.

"Yeah, we worked together a long time ago. A *long* time ago. Then that shitbag stole my idea." He told the story in an eerily gleeful manner, as if he couldn't wait for someone to ask him just the right question. It was clear that his story had become the wallpaper of his recent life. He and Mango had briefly been lovers, then friends. They came up with the basic idea of a bingo hosted by Mango as a drag queen, together. Over time, the show grew bigger, every year they added some new aspect, the live boys, the volleyball-sized equipment, all of it. Then about three years into it, Mango decided that Chester was taking too big a share of the profits, even though the split was exactly what they'd agreed upon. A long war ensued as to whom owned the rights to the show. Lawsuits and countersuits were filed in federal court over the trademark issue. Chester failed to secure an injunction, and the show was allowed to go on at the other bar, but all the proceeds excluding payroll and expenses were put into an escrow account with the court. Chester had just won in the lower court, and the only remaining question was whether Mango's lawyers would appeal.

"So I didn't need to kill nobody. I ain't sorry, he was a shitbag to me, like I said. But I won." Chester was poking himself in the chest so hard he could have bruised his own heart.

"When's the last time you talked to him?" Drew was fanning the smoke away with her legal pad.

"Not in years. Got lawyers for that. Real expensive ones." Chester crossed his beefy arms across his chest just above his considerable beer gut.

"This town is about as big as a minute. Sure about that? Sure you haven't talked to him in years? Not at all? Not even a little? If you have, it would be better if we found that out now and not from somebody else," Stephen said.

"Not at all." Chester was adamant. "Now I got a bar to run." Chester opened the door, the whoosh of air swept the smoke in a funnel. Drew and Stephen sat immersed in it like two shish kebabs on a Webber grill.

"What a lovely specimen. And people still have the nerve to ask me why I'm not married to one of those." Drew was wiping her eyes as she and Stephen made their way down Commercial.

"Really. How come gay Darwinism hasn't taken care of that guy yet? The more he talked, the more I was convinced my theory may be the right one. What about you?"

"Well, it filled in a few of the pieces. The money going into escrow explains why Mango would take a side job at the bank. And it's clear there's a long solid stream of animosity between them. People do kill for money. No question." Drew's eyes were still watering from the smoke.

"I think you're a little behind on pop culture. These days, people kill for a pair of sneakers or just the bragging rights. That guy seems a bit of a contrast, though. On the one hand, he presents personally as a blobby dumb guy, but he owns what appears to be a really lucrative business. And what about the number? Think he's binary number guy?"

"No. But he does seem to have a Teamster-like personality, if you know what I mean. He could be our connection to the Boston mob. Maybe the business is a front or a money-laundering operation. I can't begin to imagine how much cash changes hands in one night at that place. The real question we need answered is which way this points—a series of random events and two separate unrelated murders, or is it straight-up mob start to finish. How do we figure that out? Unless one of the Baychamp boys spills it, all we really have left is a number and a shoe."

"Did we get that yet, by the way? The shoe?" Stephen's voice trailed off as he shot across the street and stopped in front of Glint, a small bar in the downstairs space of Rope 'Em and Ride 'Em, a sex toy emporium. "Hey listen, Drew, I know that song." Stephen waved her over to the bar. "Listen, it's the Bettes. Cool, let's go in. Just for one drink."

"That doesn't sound like Betty to me. I don't think they'd be playing a venue this small. Not for years now." Drew followed behind him down a short, narrow set of stairs.

"Not Betty. The Bettes. The Alpha Bettes, you know, 'I Spent

My Last Ten Dollars on Birth Control and Beer.'" Stephen opened the door and gave the bouncer two five-dollar bills.

"I thought Two Nice Girls did that song." Drew shouted the order of one Rolling Rock and one Diet Coke to the bartender.

"They did, like fifteen years ago. But the Alpha Bettes just covered it. It's huge on straight FM right now. Hey, thanks." Stephen took the Rolling Rock, and they made their way to the farthest table at the back of the bar. The bar was not that crowded, most people were still either enjoying an early dinner or still primping for a night on the town. "I'm surprised they didn't draw a bigger crowd."

"Well, it's early for this town yet. These girls are wicked cute, I'll say that much." The two acoustic rock guitarists, lead singer, and drummer were all no older than twenty-five. They were all blond, with boyish unsculpted rail-thin bodies hidden under enormous baggy hip-hugging black jeans and mid-length white T-shirts that read, "We're Not Betty."

"I love the shirts." Drew ordered a second Diet Coke and a cup of coffee.

"They're too cute. I love their look and their music. I'm a sucker for all girl bands." Stephen began air drumming on the table. "Oh, man, they're not breaking already, we just got here."

"They'll be back in like ten minutes." Drew inadvertently looked at her watch.

"I know, but this is the only fun we've...correction...I've... gotten to have on this whole trip. So spill it, sister, I saw you talking to gorgeous doctor. What's up with that?"

"She was just coming in from a swim. Lucky for me. I know I can't, ya know..."

"Play doctor? Do the wango tango? Fuck her brains out?" Stephen continued drumming even in the absence of the music.

"Lovely. Thank you so much. Yes, one of those, but she is really something. I've almost never seen the way light attaches to a woman like that. And stop doing that drumming, it's annoying the shit out of me." Drew placed her hands firmly over Stephen's.

"Oh, sorry." Stephen gripped his beer bottle with both hands. "So? There was conversation?"

"Yes. Some. Actually, we're going to dinner tomorrow night. If I have time, that is. Which reminds me, yes to your question about the shoe. Spree must have been able to find a duplicate over the Internet based on the make and model."

"The size and style?"

"Whatever. Anyway, she must have shipped it UPS because the M&Ms, or rather just one of the Ms, called earlier to see if she could sign for the package. So now at least we might have something we can work with, a shoe and a number. All we need is a plan to go with it." Drew held up her coffee cup for the bar back to refill it.

"We also have Brian Chester, don't forget."

"Stephen, I love ya to death, but I don't really think Mr. Potato Head from the Boat Dock there is of any real value. One more set here, then we really have to go." The Alpha Bettes retook the stage and started in on a punked-out cover of Leonard Cohen's "Hallelujah."

"Oh, I love this song. And don't think for one minute that I've forgotten to get the details about dinner with the doctor. There will be more questions. Many. Resistance is futile."

They smiled at each other and mouthed the words along with the band.

Chapter Twenty-four

Stephen was naked except for a pair of black boxer shorts and one black high heel. He was walking in wobbly fashion across the kitchen toward the coffeepot. Just short of the counter, his balance gave way, and he hit the linoleum with a resounding thud. The yellow plastic smiley face coffee cup skittered across the floor like a frightened kitten. Drew rounded the corner at a high rate of speed holding a can of Aquanet hair spray, her finger planted firmly on the nozzle.

"Stephen? Is this some weird secret life thing, or are you channeling Chita Rivera?"

"I'm fine, thanks for asking. At least I didn't break the heel on this." Stephen kicked off the high heel and righted himself.

"I'm sorry. That was going to be my next question. It really was. Followed quickly by, what the hell are you doing? What the hell are you doing anyway? It's like five thirty in the morning." Drew set the can of Aquanet on the counter, grabbed some paper towels, and began wiping the spilled coffee up off the floor.

"I've been up for a couple of hours, lucky for you. I have big news. The biggest. I was just waiting for you to get up. Damn, I really hurt my knee." Stephen stood up, leaned against the counter, and began examining his right knee. "And nobody, and I do mean nobody, thinks hair care is more important than I do, but I'm compelled to ask why it is you sleep with a can of hair spray. Especially when you're sleeping alone." Stephen held the can of

Aquanet in his hand. "And they have made better hair product since the seventies, you know."

"Shut up. It was in the bathroom. That's where I was when I heard the noise. I didn't know who or what was out here. That's all I could find. Now what is the big news that got you up at the crack of dawn?" Drew threw the coffee-soaked paper towels in the garbage can and set the smiley face cup in the sink.

"So you intended to make sure that the robber's hair looked good for the perp walk?"

"Funny. You are a funny, funny man. It's as good as Mace, especially if that's all you have. Now why are we up so early? And why on earth were you trying to walk in this shoe? Plus which, some pants would be good."

"Details, details. Okay, I'm getting pants and you're going to look at what's over on the table. I'm a genius. ASRE rules, sister." Stephen hobbled to the far bedroom.

"Why, what's on the table?"

"Just look," Stephen shouted from the bedroom.

Drew sat at the table and started looking through the cluster of strewn papers and small toys. There were a series of numbers and the letters d, i, n, g, o. The rest of the table was covered with miniature versions of well-known food icons. There was a Gorton's Fisherman, Snap, Crackle, and Pop, Aunt Jemima, the Lucky Charms leprechaun, the Jolly Green Giant, the Pillsbury Doughboy, the musical California Raisins, Mr. Peanut, and a red Kool-Aid smiley face pitcher. "So you're telling me the Jolly Green Giant killed him?"

"No. Look, I figured it out, I think. Why did you move those?" Stephen began rearranging the icons.

"Sorry, didn't mean to insult your little friends here. I think maybe now would be a good time to explain this."

"Okay, look. It was something about seeing the Alpha Bettes. It really stuck with me for some reason. I couldn't figure out why. I mean, I like their music, but it's nothing to keep you up at night or anything. But I couldn't really sleep, then it sort of hit me." Stephen reached for the papers on the table and started laying them out in front of Drew.

"The Alpha Bettes killed him? What are you talking about?"

"Look here. I was just juggling this number in my head over and over again, then I remembered the numbers stand for letters of the alphabet. I thought it was ASCII code."

"What's ACKY code?"

"Not ACKY, ASCII. It's used for writing computer code. For translating letters into numbers so the computer can understand it."

"How do you know all this?" Drew started examining the papers in front of her.

"Remember when I did that short-lived transfer to the cyber crime unit?"

"Oh, yeah, that was pretty funny. Remember you thought you were going to become a cyber crime genius, then go and get hired at Microsoft and make a few million dollars. I think that was right around the time they started showing reruns of 'Dynasty' on cable. But I didn't know you were over there long enough to learn how to write computer code. So these numbers make letters somehow? Is that what you're saying?"

"I didn't learn how to write it, but I did remember that's how it was done, sort of. So I called William Four, remember the guy from MIT, my brief fling with geekdom?"

"You called him after all this time in the middle of the night? Wasn't he a little freaked out by that?"

"Not really, we talk occasionally. Anyway, he confirmed this stuff for me, except he ran it through something called a base 26 converter to convert the zeros and ones to paired numbers that are then converted to letters. For him, of course, it was like first-grade stuff. Then we had phone sex. Anyway, look, it spells dingo. What do you think about that? Pretty impressive, don't you think?"

"You had phone sex?" Drew said.

"I think you might have missed the point of the story altogether. Look here on this list. Here's our number 6873787179 right. So if you separate them all out, it goes like this 68 is D, 73 is I, 78 is N and so on. Look it translates perfectly into dingo."

"I'll be damned. Look at that. So how hard is this to figure out? Does it take like a degree to know how to do this? I guess not if you figured it out. So how big's the circle on this? Just about anybody with some computer knowledge could do this? Is that what we think?"

"William seemed to think it was pretty basic stuff. Not just anybody, but somebody who had taken a few computer courses or even done some research on the Internet could probably pull this off. The question is, why would he leave a direct clue like this? Until this checked out, we were on a whole different track here. What would lead someone to point the finger at themselves? It couldn't have been for Mango's benefit, he was the victim. This guy was leaving this to warn off someone else, don't we think?"

"Yes, absolutely. So who would that be? The only other person we know of with a stake in this is the guy from the Boat Dock. What about somebody else from the show? Anything about computer experience come out in our interviews that you remember?"

"No. I checked the notes pretty carefully. I don't think we asked any questions about their backgrounds that would have given us that kind of information. I think we need to reinterview."

"So that answers one of my questions. The next is, what are all these toys doing over here? Are these yours? How bored were you anyway? And please don't tell me these had something to do with the phone sex." Drew picked up the Jolly Green Giant and pointed it toward Stephen.

"You're really stuck on that phone sex thing, aren't you? I was trying to remember all the dingo cast members and was getting confused. I thought the visuals might help. It did, too. Look." Stephen began arranging the icons on the table top.

"I just don't know why you keep going back to him, that's all. It's not like you and William Four have anything in common." Drew began rolling the Jolly Green Giant over and over with her thumb.

"That's not true. We both hate lawn ornaments." Stephen snatched the giant out of her hand and stood it in its rightful place on the table, leaned back, and admired his work. "See, this made it much easier."

"So far, this looks like a chess game on crack to me. Explain please."

"Here are all the possible dingo suspects. First, we have the least likely, the Lucky Charms, represented by, what else but the Lucky Charms leprechaun. The next least likely, the tables, Anna Rexia and Iatta Cupcake represented by the Campbell Soup Kids. Then we have Donita Facelift, Ida Slapter, Nidda Biggerone, Ginger Vitus, and Olive Inatrailer, each represented by one of the California Raisins. See I marked these little matchbook covers with the letters so we could tell them apart. This, of course, represents Lois Carmen Denominator." Stephen held up the Kool-Aid frosted smiley face pitcher. "Then finally, Kenneth, the new bar owner of Lucky, the Gorton's Fisherman, and Brian Chester, the most likely suspect still, at least in my opinion, represented by Cap'n Crunch. And voilà, the entire cast of suspects is complete."

"This seemed like a good idea at three in the morning, did it?"

"Come on. How else are we going to keep them straight? What do you think? I say we begin ranking them right now." Stephen grabbed a legal pad off the coffee table.

"I agree the tables are the least likely. They make money no matter who runs the show. So they're out." Drew placed the Campbell's Soup kids on their sides. "And the Lucky Charms, I don't think so. First, they're all too young, and it seems more like just their summer job. I can't believe any of them would have a financial stake in this. So out goes the leprechaun."

"Now on the other end of the spectrum, Mr. Brian Chester is our most likely. He has the most to lose if Mango had decided to appeal the court's ruling on the trademark, so Cap'n Crunch here goes right in the middle. I think the next most likely is one of the Dingos, Lois Carmen, or Kenneth, the new bar owner. The question is, in what order and why?"

"Kenneth, I would think, would be at the top. If Brian Chester moves that show back to the Boat Dock, Kenneth stands to lose, well, a boatload of money. Besides, he was more evasive with us than Chester was. Which means either he's hiding something or that he's just a complete asshole. Next, I would pick Lois Carmen. How did he end up getting that headliner spot anyway, do we know?" Drew moved the Kool-Aid pitcher to the center of the table.

"Not really. Something about knowing the bar owner. He said they hadn't made a decision about who would get the headline spot permanently. He said the bar owner wanted someone from the outside to keep the Dingos from fighting over it. So that leaves them actually, the Dingos." Stephen grabbed all five California Raisins and moved them to the center of the table.

"The Dingos? Really? None of those guys seemed much like killer drag queens to me. They just stand there most of time, and during breaks, they each do a song. Seems to me like they're just using that to advertise their own shows."

"But what if one of them wanted to have the coveted Mango spot, center stage? Wouldn't that mean more money for them? Being the headliner?" Stephen said.

"I guess so. Certainly, whoever has that spot carries the show. Okay, let's say they're in for now. But they all have an equal stake in it. That gives at least five guys an equal motive. How are we going to winnow that down? Spree can run background checks, we can see if anybody has a criminal record or any computer experience, but beyond that, how else can we cut this list down?"

"You forget, we do have one more clue." Stephen placed the high heel down in front of Drew.

"Stephen, you can't be serious."

Chapter Twenty-five

"God loves you, and I'm working on it."

Drew and Stephen stood staring at the words written on the sign in front of the Provincetown Universalist Church, announcing the topic of the week's sermon. They were sitting on a stone bench at the front of the church, making last-minute adjustments to what neither seriously considered the master plan.

"Stephen, I can't believe I let you talk me into this. We need to rethink this. It has disaster written all over it."

"Maybe we were overtired when we developed Operation Cinderella Redux?"

"Ya think?"

"We could just do straight-up interviews as follow-ups. We have it narrowed a little bit by the background checks Spree did." Stephen started flipping through the large fax in the file on his lap.

"How narrow?" Drew began reading over his shoulder.

"Well, we calculated ten principles plus the Lucy Charms, which brings it to somewhere between fifteen and eighteen. We can eliminate the Lucky Charms, which I think we both agree are a non-starter."

"Yes. Agreed." Drew nodded.

"So really it's ten principles. Of the two most likely, Brian Chester, the Boat Dock guy, and Kenneth, the owner of Lucky, both have some computer experience but no formal training, at least that we could uncover so far."

"Please tell me Spree did more than Google these guys." Drew began ruffling the papers on Stephen's lap.

"Of course she did. She ran full background checks. Relax, will ya, and quit doing that, you're folding the edges of the papers. You know how much I hate that."

"Okay, sorry. So old bar owner, new bar owner. Okay, that's two. Next?"

"Nothing on the tables, just as we suspected. So let's just eliminate them, except as background interviews. So now we're down to six, Lois Carmen Denominator and the five Dingo girls." Stephen drew eight circles on the fax cover sheet.

"Right. What about Lois Carmen? She seems to have gained the most prominence so far. She gets paid a higher cut, too, at least two percent more than the other guys. That could add up to a lot over time. What about computer experience?"

"Yes, I agree. Some computer classes in community college, right here on the Cape, as a matter of fact. And only two years ago." Stephen handed the background papers on Lois to Drew."

"I didn't know there even was a community college here. So three classes in programming. According to Mr. Reach Out and Touch Me, that would be enough, right? Money can be a powerful motive. She gets a star there." Stephen drew a star around the first circle and marked it with the initials LCD.

"Just can't let the phone sex thing go, can we? Okay, so now look at the rest of the Dingos. First, Donita Facelift is definitely out. Trust fund baby."

"Really?"

"Big-time. Daddy is, get this, a plastic surgeon. Pretty famous one, too, out on the coast."

"That explains the name."

"We can't eliminate her altogether because it could be a play for attention, as well. But if we're playing the odds, I'd say she's a long shot. So let's X her for now." Stephen drew an X through the next circle and added a note, don't need a facelift 'cause I got a trust fund."

"What about Ida Slapter? I have to say, I really love that name.

So I see nothing in her background about computer stuff. She was an English lit major and from Brown. That probably means some family money, too, although it doesn't say that. But Brown costs a fortune. You just know how happy mommy and daddy are now about spending all that money on that right fine education."

"Well, what did they expect? An English literature major. Even from Brown, that's a one-way ticket to retail. Okay, she gets an X, too, then, right?" Stephen began marking the next circle.

"Stephen."

"Next."

"Stephen."

"Next."

"Stephen."

"Yes, yes, we know, you studied English lit. Homer, Iliad, Odyssey, all those dead Irish guys. We know. We just don't have time for that right now."

"I'm just saying."

"Well, so am I. Now Nidda Biggerone, and can we just say who doesn't? She's a maybe with a lean toward no. First of all, no computer experience and second, way too old. No chance she's taking over the show, murder or no murder."

"Why not?"

"I don't know, it's just too *All About Eve* in reverse. So definitely no for now."

"I'll just pretend I know what that means. But if that's the standard, then Ginger Vitus is definitely out. She looks way too much like her name. So X her out, too. This isn't leaving much. That just leaves O. Olive Inatrailer." Drew began shuffling down in the stack of papers. "Wait, we must have forgotten one. There's no sheet on her."

"I know. Spree said she came up empty on that one. The Social Security number didn't show anything. Maybe we wrote it down wrong."

"Maybe. That means she stays on the list for now. So we have the two owners, Lois Carmen, and Olive Inatrailer.

"So what's the plan exactly?"

"I think it's called Operation Hope Someone Confesses."

Drew made the sign of the cross.

"Haven't seen you do that in a long time."

"I think the theme of this whole trip for me is 'things you haven't done in a long time.' Let's go, they're waiting. And whatever you do, don't forget that shoe."

Chapter Twenty-six

Out of costume, the members of Dingo appeared indistinguishable from a meeting of the chamber of commerce in Squeebado, Wisconsin. They were sitting in the first two rows of the performance space, Lois Carmen was telling some story involving a lot of exaggerated hand gestures and head shaking.

"Stephen, I know we're not that intimidating, but don't you think it's a little weird that these guys aren't just a little more sober or nervous about this?"

"Are you kidding? It would scare the shit out of me if I thought you were coming to interview me. Maybe the cops didn't tell them what they were here for."

"Or maybe worst of all, they're all innocent. Wouldn't that totally suck?"

"That's an unsettling observation." Stephen reached in his case and took out the shoe.

"Notice how even though we spent all that time this morning, we still don't really have a plan of attack?"

"Speak for yourself, sister. Follow me." Stephen walked briskly up the center aisle until he reached the stage. He placed the black shoe in the center of the stage, then turned to address the crowd. "I take it you all know why you're here. We have spoken to most of you once already. We're just doing some follow-up interviews to clear up a few details. Some of you we will talk to individually and some in small groups to speed this along."

"Know who killed him yet?" The voice was from one of the young Lucky Charms, sitting, legs splayed in the second row.

"And you are?" Stephen said.

"Scott Seymor. What's yours?"

"Stephen Shaunessey, from—"

"Washington. We know." the first row said in unison.

"Sorry, guess everyone knows you except me," Seymor said.

"No problem." Stephen began to address the crowd again. "Anyway, this shouldn't take up too much of your tanning time. If I could get the Lucky Charms to gather in that far corner over there, that's as good a starting point as any."

"Don't we get lawyers, too?" Seymor interrupted.

"Lawyers? These are just informational interviews. Do you think you need a lawyer?"

"I think I get one whatever you think about it. You never know when an informational interview can turn into a custodial arrest. I think you shoulda told us we can have lawyers." Seymor got out of his chair and walked toward the stage, stood in front of Stephen, and folded his arms across his chest.

"Let me guess. Law student?" Stephen said.

"Harvard, the worst. We been listening to his yappin' all summer." Nidda Biggerone waved her hand in the air in the ultimate dismissive diva gesture.

"Nothing sadder than an old queen with a green streak," Seymor said to Nidda.

"Jealous? Of that?" Nidda looked Seymor up and down. "I may be old, honey, but I can still kick your scrawny little ass."

"Okay, okay. Maybe we could get back to the task at hand here and continue this fight later," Stephen said.

"Could we? Some of us have our own shows this afternoon. So shut up, Seymor, and sit the fuck down." Donita Facelift was tapping her foot furiously on the floor.

"Yes, we wouldn't want the six people who still come to see your show to be disappointed, now would we?" Seymor shot back.

"Oh, no, you didn't. I know you didn't just say that to me. She may be old..." Donita pointed at Nidda. "...but you better know

I'm South Side. I'll kick your ass so hard those robin's egg-sized white boy balls you got, you be wearing as earrings. You better back off, boy, while you still can."

"Give the kid a break, will ya? He's just a kid. Kinda cute, I think. Trying to stand up for his little white boy self." Ginger Vitus crossed her legs over and under.

"Stay out of it, Ginger. Way out of it. You wouldn't think he was so cute if you knew he called you Misfortune Cookie, now would you?" Donita said to Ginger.

"What?" Ginger stood up next to Donita. "You little puke. I got your Harvard right here." Ginger grabbed her crotch.

"Don't be pointing that at me, I ain't no rice queen," Seymor said to Ginger.

Ginger lunged forward, slipped, and fell flat on her face. Her lip began to bleed. Seymor laughed. Ginger reached out, grabbed his foot, and pulled him down. He in turn rolled onto Donita's foot, whereupon she began to kick him in the stomach. The others joined in an attempt to pull the three of them apart. Chairs began to fly. It was a full on brawl.

"Oh, my god. What are you doing? Get up. You're ruining the seating. Stop it. Get up. You crazy bitches are going to ruin my show." The loud voice came from the stage. It was Prozac Barbie. She was holding a large cardboard cutout of herself. She walked back and replaced the one of Lois Carmen Denominator. The whole scene on the floor slowed to a halt.

"What the fuck do you think you're doing up there?" Lois Carmen extricated herself from the group on the floor and stood up, hands firmly planted on her hips.

Barbie walked to the edge of the stage with the cutout of Lois. "It's easy. I'm young, you're old. So very, very old. I'm in. You're out. And don't act so surprised. You knew this gig was only temporary till I could close out my own show. Here, take your personality with you." Barbie threw the cardboard cutout at Lois. For the first time, she noticed Stephen leaning against the stage. "Oh, hello again. I remember you."

Barbie turned around and began to walk back to the set. She almost tripped on the shoe Stephen had left on the stage. Barbie bent over, picked the shoe up, and turned quickly around back toward the crowd. She began waving the shoe in a menacing manner. "And quit messing with my shit. I've been looking everywhere for this." Stephen looked at Barbie. Drew looked at Stephen. Stephen looked at Drew, then back at Barbie. "Oh, shit." Barbie took off running. Exit stage left.

They found Barbie three hours later at Dream House, an Internet summer rental business she ran on the side. It didn't take much to break her. She killed Mango for the only motive older than money—love. Seems she, Mango, and Kenneth were a throuple. A couple plus one. Kenneth and Mango had started dating right after the show moved to Lucky. But once Barbie arrived in Provincetown, Kenneth became drawn to her as if they had been made for each other. Mango was none too pleased at sharing Kenneth's affection, but over time, the three came to tolerate, if not embrace, one another.

That lasted only until Kenneth started making noises about sprucing up the show with some "new blood," perhaps giving Barbie a starring role of some kind. Barbie's own show had proven very popular among the tourists, and Kenneth wanted to try to capitalize on that.

The bank robbery had given Barbie her opening. She knew that with Mango out of the way for good, the starring role in Dingo and Kenneth would both be hers for good. The note was simply a warning to all, including Brian Chester, that any attempt to thwart her ambition would be met with similar aggression.

Chapter Twenty-seven

Dr. Austin rode up straddling a small black Honda motorcycle, moon sparking off the highly polished chrome. She was dressed in Levi's 501s, a short cropped black leather motorcycle jacket, and candy apple red helmet with a huge decal of the British flag on each side. "Let's go, then. On with ya." She held out a battered old helmet and propped it on Drew's head.

Drew slid onto the back of the seat, saying nothing, adjusted the helmet, and held onto the back of the seat bar to steady herself. J.J. reached back without turning around, grabbed each of Drew's arms, and placed them around her waist. "Best this way, can't afford to lose you now." J.J. let loose the engine and headed out on to Bradford.

"You know, we could have walked to the boat, it's not that far," Drew shouted over J.J.'s left shoulder.

"Yes, if we were going there."

"We aren't going there?"

"Eventually. But first, we're off for a bit of adventure. Can't just stroll into adventure. You have to rush headlong into it, take it by surprise. Don't you think?"

"Uh. Sure, okay."

"That sounds convincing. You'll see."

They had ridden a much shorter distance than Drew would have thought when suddenly J.J. turned the bike to the left and veered up Pearl Street. She killed the engine in front of the house and got off the bike. "What is this, J.J.? What are we doing here?" J.J. held the bike up as Drew sat motionless.

"Come on, we're going in, then. Can't have curiosity killing this cat." J.J. reached into her pocket and produced a set of gold keys. Drew looked momentarily away from J.J. and up to the house's highest window, where "Artist" still blazed blue. She looked back and forth between the window and J.J. a few more times. She got down off the bike, placed the helmet on the seat, and began walking to the front door, convinced that any break in her motion would cause her to change her mind, run away, and dive off the nearest pier. J.J. came up behind her and unlocked the door. "It's at the very top. Up those stairs."

They climbed the three fights of old darkly stained wooden stairs in silence. Drew's head was buzzing, and she felt slightly nauseated as J.J. unlocked the door to the apartment and flicked the overhead light switch. The light did not come on. "Uh-oh, hadn't counted on that. Hope she's not out of juice. Might have had all this switched off before she left."

"Well, that's still on, so something must work." Drew pointed to the fluorescent sign. "Unless it's battery operated."

"There we are." J.J. reached down and turned on the small bedside lamp. Afraid that may be all we get, though. But come on, it's enough for a bit of a look around."

Drew stepped over the threshold into the one big room that served as the living/dining/bedroom. It was either really old or was intended to be painted a white-gray. There were only three pieces of furniture. An almost new looking white canvas-covered loveseat, a four-drawer antique or garage sale pine dresser, whose top was thick with dust, and a full-sized mattress and box spring bed set on the floor. The white bed sheets looked almost fake they were so starchly new and crisp. A bed perfectly made, not a wrinkle. The only natural light fell through the round window just above it. It looked every bit like an apartment somebody used to live in. There were no traces of its inhabitant. No books, no CDs, no photographs, no magazines, not even an old newspaper or stray scrap of paper. Nothing to give away the identity of its former owner. It likely didn't even contain a fingerprint, a stray hair, not a drop of DNA.

"J.J., is there something you want to tell me?"

"Meaning what?" J.J. was sitting on the arm of the loveseat, her black leather jacket a stark contrast to the white canvas.

"Meaning how did you get the keys to this place?" Drew continued walking around the small space in the same small circle.

"Meaning have I always had the keys to this place? That the real question?"

"Well?"

"Knew you'd think that. Can't just believe I wasn't shagging her, can you? Got the keys from my friend Judy. Last night at dinner. I was talking about you and all this." J.J. swept her arm across the room. "And Judy, as it is, has been keeping half an eye on it for her. So I swindled the keys out of her. Just for tonight. Thought you deserved a peek at least."

"You were talking about me at dinner to a friend of yours?" Drew looked at J.J. with her head cocked and her left eyebrow raised.

"Well, don't be too all over yourself about it, love. You came right after the new Indigo Girls CD and just before all the talk about who's getting on with who in our small circle." J.J. smiled and folded her arms across her chest. "But yes, you were a topic. And so here we are."

"I see. So not much point in your friend Judy taking care of this place unless she's coming back to it after London." Drew walked to the tiny closet at the farthest end of the apartment and opened the door a tiny crack.

"Can't say about that. Rent's paid till the end of the season. Can't say about the rest. Mother England just might decide to keep her. I'll let you color in those lines. Something interest you in there?"

Drew had stepped partway into the closet. It held several bare black wire hangers and one navy blue tattered wool sweater. She reached out and held the fabric lightly between her fingers. She fingered it a few more times, then gently brought it up to her face and breathed it in. She breathed it in again, then dropped the sleeve sharply as if it had injured her. "This isn't hers."

"What? What isn't hers?" J.J. walked the length of the room in four short bounds.

"This sweater. This isn't Maggie's." Drew held the sweater, still on its hanger in front of her at a distance.

"How do you know? She could have bought it here, you know. Does get breezy here at night." J.J. walked around to look at Drew.

"No. It's definitely not hers. Maggie always smelled like... never mind. It's just not hers is all. Must not be. It's the only thing left here." Drew held the sweater out to J.J.

"Oh, well, I've been looking everywhere for that." J.J took the sweater off the hanger and threw it over her shoulder. "Right you are, then, it's not hers, it's mine." Drew stared at J.J. as if she had suddenly discovered her to be a kidnapper. "What? It's my sweater is all I'm saying, so mystery solved on that one." Drew said nothing, eyes on the sweater. "Oh, I see you've written your own ending again. Well, you've got it all tangled 'round, I'm afraid. I used this the day of the shooting; it was bloody freezing in here. Must have left it behind. Surprised she didn't mention it, though."

"What? What shooting? There was a shooting in here? J.J., what are you talking about?"

"I mean shooting, shooting the photos with all the fancy cameras. The photo. The photo over my bed. It was bloody freezing in here. I thought your Maggie had gone completely off it that day. Till she showed me the photo, of course. Then I had to admit, it was dead on sexy. Every hair on my body is standing on end." Drew began to look around the room again. As each piece sharpened into focus, it became clear to her. She walked over and sat gingerly on the side of the bed as if it were a delicate sculpture she might break.

"Of course. I see it now. This is where the picture was taken. The light from that window, the shape of the shadows across her body in the picture." Drew sat motionless on the side of the bed for several minutes. There was a soft buzz in her head and her foot began to throb a little, the Ace bandage suddenly felt excruciatingly tight. She bent and attempted some adjustment. She began to fall forward. J.J. caught her by the shoulders.

"What's wrong? Come on now, lie back."

"I don't know, all of a sudden, this bandage feels really too tight. It's throbbing like mad."

J.J. pushed Drew's head gently onto the pillow, raised her injured foot, and set it gently on a pillow in her lap. "Feel like you've a separate heart in here beating all on its own?" Drew grimaced and nodded. "Well, it is wrapped too tight. This isn't how I wrapped it. You're lucky there's any circulation left in here at all. Did you do this?"

"Stephen."

"Oh, a doctor now, is he? Always trying to undo all my good work. Lie back and be still, if that's at all possible, while I loosen this a wee bit." J.J.'s touch was almost imperceptibly soft as she made several adjustments to the bandage. When she finished, she slowly ran her fingers up over Drew's foot to her ankle. She grasped Drew's foot lightly in her hands and made small circles. "Hurt when I do that, does it?"

"No, actually. The throbbing is subsiding quite a bit now." Drew lay on the bed and watched J.J. make several more small circles until she began to feel that familiar and terrifying feeling leaping in her stomach. "Okay, that's good. You don't need to keep doing that now. It's all better." Drew attempted to sit up.

"Wouldn't do that quite yet." J.J. reached up and gently held her palm to Drew's breastbone until she was lying flat on the bed once more. "Give it a few more minutes until the blood begins to recirculate. Otherwise, it's likely to just start up again."

"I'm sorry. This isn't turning out to be much of a gratitude dinner for you so far. I guess I owe you two after tonight. Good thing there's more than one good restaurant in this town now."

"Well, night's not over quite yet. Although, if this foot doesn't improve a great deal in the next few, I'm recommending a long stretch of bed rest. You needn't feed me out of gratitude, although I must say, when you're about, I do feel a somewhat persistent hunger." J.J. broke into a broad toothy smile.

"Uh-huh. I'm certain you do. That's what appetizers are for.

Appetizers in the crowded restaurant we're going to in like ten minutes. I promise you can have all you want. It's on me." Drew shifted her eyes quickly off J.J. and began to scan the room again in rapid fashion. "I have to say, it's more than a little weird being here like this. Makes me feel a little bit like a home invader or something."

"Feel like you're invading her privacy, do you?"

"Well, no. I mean, not exactly. I don't really know this place as hers. It just doesn't really register that way with me. Just seems like a stark, empty place where nothing much really happened. Nothing I know about anyway. Which is both incredibly irritating and just as well, I suppose. I cleaned out one house. Sort of. I don't need the burden and uncertainty of another."

"Well, you know one thing that happened here." J.J. suddenly stood up on the bed. The motion created almost a wave in the mattress, and Drew's attention was drawn back to J.J., who was attempting to keep a steady balance while standing over her.

"Are you going to do a cheer? Or what's the deal here?"

"It was a bit like this." J.J. ever so gently placed one foot at the very crux of Drew's hipbone and lightly lifted herself. Her arms were stretched out at her sides like a tightrope walker's and lifted up and down in jittery sudden movements as she attempted to keep her balance. "This was the hardest part, took forever to get this right."

Drew laughed a little at first, unsure exactly what was happening. "What the hell are you doing? If you fall on my foot, I'm going to kill you. Get down from there before you break your own self."

After a few more minutes of sudden jerky, almost falling off moments, J.J. finally steadied herself on her one leg. "Once you have that down, the rest is easy." J.J. arched her other foot and brought it down just at the hem of Drew's shirt. She slowly began insinuating her toes underneath, lifting the fabric, but barely.

"Get down. Now. As in right now." J.J. was lost to her balancing and the path her toes were headed. "If you think I won't throw you off, you don't know me."

After a brief detente, J.J. lowered herself with care, until her knees were straddling Drew's hips on the bed. Silence. Calculations. Risk. Reward. J.J. bent slowly forward with the care of a ballerina until she was close enough to Drew's mouth that they shared breath. They lay six or seven minutes in this slow tense teeter-totter of inhale-exhale. Then J.J. attempted a light kiss. Drew turned her face, left, right, left with J.J. chasing. "J.J., stop it." She tried to raise herself up on her elbows, gain some leverage. "Stop it. I can't." She felt one arm, then the other being pulled above her head in one swift motion. J.J. held her as fiercely as muscle holds memory. Inhale, exhale, inhale, exhale, inhale. Finally, Drew raised her head and delivered an astonishing, shattering kiss.

They fucked like cave girls. An electric swarm of fingers, teeth, tongue, the smell of salt, sweat, leather, the bitter accidental taste of metal. Fabric crinkling, then tearing, buckles, belts rattling, shoes thudding against wood, waistbands, fingers, the sudden feel of endless skin, the urgency of exposure, a cacophony of need, bodies sliding together, apart, tickling, burning, tongues, teeth, fingers opening, one, two, three, four. Face down, two arms around a waist, hips being raised, a firm skimming of rough fingernails, brilliantly shaped syllables escaped in a stream, trailing hard kisses down a backbone, tongue, hand, no, object, slick and hard as marble, resistance, insistence, resistance, insistence, patterns formed on the wall, shadows on a collision course, a gathering rhythm, fists grasping at sheets, resistance, insistence, power arcing upward, tongue, object, tongue, object, power arcing upward, the mysterious music of muscles gathering, release rising, a sharp insistent fluttering, release rising, an exquisite trembling, release rising, a thousand white balloons ascending, bodies releasing their secrets in a fierce, primal baptism, a ridiculous number of angels drumming a steady, ebbing beat until they fell away one by one holding their round bellies in fits of sighs and giggles.

Chapter Twenty-eight

They met the next morning at Crumbles for the breakfast Stephen would forever refer to after that as "bacon and legs." Drew downed three cups of coffee in less than three minutes. J.J. dipped her finger in her cappuccino and licked the white froth from her finger.

"Just Cheerios please. And some more coffee when you get a chance would be great." Drew sipped the last of her coffee.

"Three eggs over lightly, a tall stack of blueberry pancakes, a sesame bagel lightly toasted, real butter please, and a slice of that good-looking orange melon." J.J. handed the waitress her menu.

"Wow."

"Haven't had a meal since yesterday afternoon. Guess I'll have to travel to your capital to make good on that dinner I'm still owed. No appetite for you then? For food or conversation? We've just a wee bit of time here. Or shall I just watch you gobble all that caffeine till your heart bursts?"

"Oh, my god, this is caffeinated? No wonder my heart is racing. I'm sorry."

"Racing, is it?" J.J. reached across the table and placed two fingers around Drew's wrist. "You'll live. Sorry about what? Best to clarify that right off, I'd say."

"Oh, not about that. Not about last night. I mean about being less than good company."

"You're fine company. Can't see how anybody can be, really,

this bloody early in the morning." The waitress set the enormous platters of food down in front of J.J. "Now here's a reason to get up in the morning. Eat something. You must be as famished as I am, unless you and your boyfriend went to Spiritus for pizza last night after you dashed away." J.J. pushed the plate full of pancakes in Drew's direction.

"Dashed away? Yes, I guess I did sort of do that, didn't I? I never thought of myself as much of a dasher actually, but yes, that's about right. So I should explain that. I was just a little freaked out, that's all. First, all that happened yesterday with the case, then the apartment. You sort of just sprung that on me, you know?" Drew carved through the pancakes with her fork.

"My fault then, is it?"

"No. I'm not saying that. I'm just saying I wasn't expecting that. It was a lot to take in."

"You can stop now. A simple 'sorry I dashed away, but here I am now' will suffice nicely. You Americans get way too tangled 'round in your apologies. It was just a wrinkle in time, no one is proposing marriage. Even if it is all the rage. Not every star's for wishing on, some are for momentary illumination only. Don't spend much time looking in the rearview mirror myself, that's only for backing up or parking. I'm more an eyes forward person, eyes on the road, never know what's coming 'round the bend and all that. I'll take questions now, I know you have some." J.J. pushed the last plate away from her to the center of the table.

"You are a very strange woman."

"You, on the other hand, are a cakewalk, I think it is. That right? Cakewalk?"

"Yes. Cakewalk. And okay, I do have many questions, but one I would really like answered while I'm still here. What the hell was that thing you used last night? It was, well, incredible."

J.J. smiled. "Of all the questions, that's the most important, is it?" She reached into her jacket pocket, pulled it out, and set it down in front of Drew. "It's a fossil. Found it on the beach. Was going to add it to my collection, but as you can see, this one has a keen shape." Drew ran her hand lightly over the object.

"Wow, it's so..."

"Yes, it is. Once they're oxidized by the sea, they become like soapstone, smooth to the touch but hard as marble. It's ancient by the look of it. Seemed a shame to waste it only for looking at. Besides, that kind of staying power, being swallowed by the sea, then birthed out again should be celebrated in some way, wouldn't you agree?" J.J. pushed the object toward Drew. "Here, you take it with you, then. All yours. A souvenir. Won't find that in your average tourist shop. Best get on with it now or you'll miss your flight and your boyfriend will be having attitude with me on his cellular."

"He's not my boyfriend."

"Have it your way. Relationships come in all flavors, can't always tell by the packaging. Anyway, we best be off." They got up from the table. J.J. reached over and handed Drew the fossil.

"Thank you."

"It's for the best anyway. Couldn't possibly think of using it again. Don't think anyone could live up to those expectations." J.J. reached down and touched the object lightly. "Not perfectly sure, but I think you've had as much as a thousand years of survival deep within you now."

Chapter Twenty-nine

"Jesus, how are we supposed to go back to the regular boring world now?" Stephen peered down at the dunes as the light plane lifted off.

"Oh, you forget, Washington has its own freaky people."

"Yes, but they're all elected. I must say, though, those Tippi girls were something else. I ran into them again last night. And you? Dating a doctor. Mother's so proud of you." Stephen crossed his hands over his heart.

"We aren't dating."

"You aren't? Oh. Sorry."

"Well, don't be. Not every star is for wishing on, some only provide momentary illumination."

"Oh, look, it's Yodel."

"It's not Yodel, it's Yoda. Plus which, shut up." Drew hit Stephen halfway hard on the arm.

"Ow. Sorry never saw it." Stephen loosened his seat belt.

"You never saw *Star Wars*? You never saw Princess Leia?"

"No. And I'm not interested in Princess Leia. I'm interested in Princess Laid You. Spill it, sister."

"It was the best sex I've had since Maggie."

"It's the only sex you've had since Maggie."

"But still."

"Was it hard having sex again? After all that time? Was it hard?"

"Let's just say, if she came in bottles, we'd be taking a case of her home with us."

About the author

Originally from Chicago, where she was a member of *SoPo Writers* and was publisher of the *Queer Planet Review*, Allison Nichol has been widely published in journals such as *The Pegasus Review*, *The Rockford Review*, *Common Lives/Lesbian Lives*, *The Evergreen Chronicles*, and *Folio* and the anthologies *Dykes With Baggage: A Lighter Look at Lesbians and Therapy* (Alyson Publications 2000), *Family Celebrations* (Andrews McMeel, 1999), *Reclaiming the Heartland, Gay and Lesbian Voices from the Midwest* (University of Minnesota Press, 1996), and *A loving Testimony: Remembering Loved Ones Lost to AIDS*, (Crossing Press, 1995).

Her poetry has been adapted for the stage and featured on Chicago's *Dial-A-Poem*.

She is a longtime civil rights lawyer now working in Washington, D.C., where she lives with her partner of seventeen years. This is her first novel.

Other Titles from
Intaglio Publications
www.intagliopub.com

You can purchase other Intaglio
Publications books online at
www.bellabooks.com, www.scp-inc.biz, or at
your local book store.

Published by
Intaglio Publications
Walker, LA

Visit us on the web
www.intagliopub.com